THE
PARTNERSHIP

THE
PARTNERSHIP

CHARLES BUTLER

Boxtree

First published in the UK 1991
by BOXTREE LIMITED, 36 Tavistock Street,
London WC2E 7PB

1 3 5 7 9 10 8 6 4 2

TM & © 1991 Twentieth Century Fox Film Corporation

ISBN: 1 85283 601 6

Photoset by Rowland Phototypesetting Limited,
Bury St Edmunds, Suffolk

Printed and bound in Great Britain by Cox & Wyman Ltd,
Reading, Berks.

A catalogue record for this book is available from the
British Library

1

Margaritas at Malibu

Arnie Becker planned a quiet evening at home. A couch potato – that's what he wanted to be. Not every night, not even every week; but tonight the idea appealed to him. He would ignore the contents of his briefcase and pretend he didn't have a high-powered job. Blot out the pressures of clients and office, and just relax by himself. What was the point of paying a fortune for this apartment if he never spent any time there?

He'd already hired a video – a movie he'd been meaning to see but had missed first time around – and bought a six-pack of low-alcohol beer. His hand was just reaching out for the telephone, to order a home-delivery deep pan pizza, when it rang.

'Hi, this is Sally. Is that you, Arnie?'

'Yeah. Sally *who*?'

'Sally Petersen. Don't you remember me?'

'Oh, sure. Sally Petersen.' Becker riffled through his brain cells trying to place her. 'How are you?' he said, playing for time.

'Terrific. It's just that I need some help . . .' She paused.

'What?' The dreadful thought occurred that this might be a former client wanting professional advice out of office hours. But how had she got his home number?

His voice must have shown concern, for her tone became reassuring.

'Oh, nothing serious. It's just that I wondered if you'd like to come to a party.'

Still unable to put a face to her, but equally unable to resist continuing the conversation, Becker said, 'Sure. When?'

'Tonight.'

'But it *is* tonight. Like, it's 7.30.'

'I know. It's too bad I couldn't give you more notice. Especially as we haven't seen each other in ages.'

At last, a lead. 'Yes, it has been a long time. When was it, exactly? The last time we saw each other, I mean.'

'Oh, you *must* remember.' Her voice lingered over the vowels. 'That wonderful night – the benefit ball at the Getty Museum. It was all in Roman costume.'

Becker gulped. Suddenly he remembered all too well, especially the moment when his toga had assumed a mind of its own and collapsed in a heap around his feet, leaving him standing almost naked among the statues. Only minutes earlier he had been admiring his aquiline profile in an antique mirror, thinking how well the flowing costume suited him. He'd been far too embarrassed to call Sally again after that.

'Yeah, sure I remember. Wish I didn't in some ways.'

'You were wonderful. All the girls admired your physique. Anyway, would you like to join me tonight?'

Becker recalled Sally's long legs and slightly protruding teeth – unusual in a city where visits to orthodontists begin almost at birth. Maybe she was from out of town. As far as he could remember, the legs kind of cancelled out the teeth anyway. Further than that he hadn't got and he thought he'd like to check out the other parts of her body, so he said, 'OK. Where shall we meet?'

He could watch the video later if she didn't make out.

*

8

BOOM – ba – da . . . DOOM – ba – da . . . BOOM – ba – da. Oliver Stone's movie about Jim Morrison had made The Doors fashionable again and the volume was turned way up.

'Great music!' Arnie shouted.

'What?'

'Oh, forget it.' He gave in to the waves of sound competing with the waves pounding on the beach. Then someone put on the old 'Woodstock' album and he felt as though he were drowning in nostalgia. He folded his arms around Sally's gyrating body and held her close. She was wearing a tight black dress of some slippery material that made it hard for him to get a grip.

'What a great party!' he whispered in her ear. He meant it too. Who'd want to be a couch potato on a night like this? The only trouble was, he felt over-dressed in his well-cut suit.

The party was at a swanky beach house on Malibu. One of those places that look like a shack from the road, but on the inside it was done up like a 1930's movie set, complete with a white grand piano and a bar the size of a counter at Nieman-Marcus.

Some guy in the record business was giving the party. Sally said he was called Adrian Calvados and that he'd originally come from Birmingham, England. Becker couldn't tell which one he was, since most of the men seemed to be dressed in one of two uniforms – designer denims and a lot of heavy, ugly gold jewellery, trying to hold in their paunches and pretending they were ten years younger; while the others wore more formal clothes but had taken off their jackets and loosened their ties, workaholic yuppies who'd come straight on from their offices. One of these even held a mobile telephone to his ear, trying to conduct a conversation above the deafening music.

All the girls looked alike, with identical hairstyles. They all had long, tanned legs, short skirts, tiny bottoms and very white humourless smiles. Even their noses were the same shape – maybe a plastic surgeon had given discount for quantity. At least Sally's nose was her own.

'Why did you call me?' he asked her. 'I mean, I'm glad you did but it was kinda late.'

Sally looked embarrassed. 'Rock's wife called. His ex-wife, I mean. She's having some kind of crisis. She and her kids were in hysterics. The man she's been living with just walked out on her.'

'So then Rock walked out on you? That doesn't seem fair. Who's Rock, anyway?'

'Oh, this guy I've been dating. Nothing serious. What happened this evening has turned me right off him anyway. But I really wanted to come to this bash and I hate going to parties on my own.'

'And so you went through your little black book until you got to me?'

'I didn't have to go very far,' Sally said candidly. 'Your surname starts with B, after all.'

Arnie wondered why people kept wandering indoors when it was so great outside. A warm velvet night: and for once the sky was clear and he could even see some stars above the Pacific. Perhaps, he thought, stars had been at a premium this year in L.A. because somebody hadn't kept up the payments. After all, everything had a price in this city. So why not the stars?

The swordfish grilling on the barbeque smelt good, and drink was being lavishly dispensed from a table near the beach house. He sipped his second margarita and put his arm around Sally again.

'I'm pleased it doesn't begin with Z; then maybe you wouldn't have called me.'

Sally smiled. Her teeth didn't look as crooked as they had the night of the Roman party. Maybe she'd had them straightened. She really was cute, he thought: and, with luck, might turn out to have slightly more grey cells inside her skull than most of the bimbos here.

Arnie Becker kissed her briefly and decided to save the rest for later. The anticipation of unfolding her long brown legs and exploring further made him his blood quicken.

'Let's eat,' he said, his mouth watering at the thought of swordfish followed by sex.

2

Hi, I'm a Scorpio

'Hi! My name's Nina. What's your sign? I'm Scorpio.'

A red-haired girl wafted through the darkness and stood in front of Becker, swaying provocatively. He smiled and muttered something. He could never remember his sign and didn't care anyway.

Arnie could detect the smell of marijuana as she stood near him, and he was suddenly reminded of his college days – making him suddenly feel twenty years younger.

'What do you do?' she asked, shouting against the insistent beat of the music.

'I'm an attorney,' he said, suddenly picking up those lost twenty years again.

'An *attorney*!' she shrieked, making him temporarily deaf in one ear. 'That's real cute! D'ya get people sent to prison?'

'No. I'm a divorce lawyer.'

'A *divorce lawyer*? But that's just great! I wish you could divorce me!'

'What do you do?' he yelled at her in turn.

'I'm a psychic chiropodist!'

'A *what*?'

'I tell people's future from looking at their feet. I work with a lot of movie stars. It's very challenging work.'

'I bet it is!' he said enthusiastically, noticing her free-flowing bosom under her dress.

'As well as chiropody,' she went on, 'I do reflexology and Shiatsu. You can tell everything about a person from their feet!' She flung her arms wide and her voluminous purple dress fluttered around her, like dark sensual flames.

15

Becker didn't know quite what to say. He rarely did at parties – unless there were a lot of other grey-suited attorneys to talk to. Anyway, this girl Nina was no more flaky than half the population of California. Yet he felt hemmed in even though there was plenty of room on the beach. If the girl were really psychic, she'd realise she was crowding him.

The conversation swirled round him, disjunctive, meaningless, booming off his eardrums as everybody competed to be heard.

'It's kinda depressing because she's not in love with her . . .'

'They've got this fantastic ongoing relationship, but they're not gay . . .'

'I find I drink far more now I'm married . . .'

'Yah, and I been walking around in a daze ever since . . .'

'I hear he goes ape-shit sometimes. Has these nervous breakdowns . . .'

'Let's swim,' Nina said, her lips grazing his ear. 'Then I'll give you a free Shiatsu session.' She was already lifting her dress over her head, her hips moving luxuriantly in time to the rhythmic beat.

'Hey, wait a minute!' Becker exclaimed, determined to keep his own clothes on, especially his shoes and socks. He didn't feel quite ready to have a strange naked woman fondling his feet and telling him he'd live to a great age and become incredibly rich and sit on the Supreme Court but must beware of anyone who was Libra . . .

'Where's Sally?' he said, in mild panic. 'She might want to swim too.'

Normally, the idea of an attractive girl stripping off would have appealed to him; but he also liked his erotic pleasures served up with some delicacy, and in private. Here things seemed to be getting out of hand. He looked round and saw people throwing off their clothes, leaving them where they fell, and plunging into the lazy white surf with shrieks of excitement.

He watched one magnificent creature – a statuesque blonde whose tanned body showed no white bikini marks. She was followed into the water by a squat dark man, naked except for dark glasses and a heavy gold chain round his neck, with tufts of thick black hair on his shoulders and down the hollow of his back. He looked to Arnie like a huge piece of half-chewed toffee that had been picked up off a dark-pile carpet.

Then there was another naked woman, as tall as a beanpole, and so thin she looked like something out of an ad for famine relief.

That was the trouble, Arnie thought. Who'd pay good money to join in an orgy with guys like that? Who'd do it for free, for that matter?

Nina, who was now standing naked at his side, said, 'Just look at that thin woman! Jeeze, looks like she's been overdoing the Jane Fonda routine! D'ya like 'em thin, Arnie?'

'Not like that,' he said. 'It'd be like going to bed with a needle!'

She gave a shriek of hysterical laughter. There was altogether too much laughter, staccato, uninhibited, pointless; he was reminded of a children's party slipping out of control.

From the direction of the beach house the shrieks were now getting louder. Arnie thought he heard a whistle, keen and clear on the night air. Then out of the darkness familiar figures materialised. All too familiar – although Arnie usually only saw them in the line of duty, from the right side of the law.

Suddenly the beach was crowded. A harsh voice sounded through a megaphone: *'Everybody stay where you are! This is the police! nobody move! You are surrounded!'*

Panic ensued. Half-naked figures tried to cover themselves; some tried making a dash for it along the sands; others dived back into the ocean; while a few – like Arnie – walked resignedly back towards the beach house.

Inside the open french windows the quadrophonic music was like a relentless artillery barrage. More naked or near-naked figures were curled up on sofas, sprawled out on sheepskin rugs, entwined, so it seemed, in all the permutations of the Karma Sutra, so that Arnie was reminded of that Dorothy Parker dictum: *If all the girls here were laid end to end, I wouldn't be at all surprised.*

The room was almost dark, the air heavy with an acrid bittersweet smell. There were police at all the doors, and a police car and three police transit vans on the road outside. There were also a number of policewomen, some of whom looked even tougher than their male colleagues.

A girl with flaming hair, wearing only black lace panties, lay sprawled back on the floor, screaming with laughter at the sight of the policewomen helping to make arrests. 'Hey, just look at those crazy dudes! They got guns an' all!'

'This a fancy dress party?' someone yelled.

Arnie had noticed that all the police, the women included, were wearing the flaps of their holsters unbuttoned; and that those standing at the doors were clasping their night-sticks at the ready.

More and more police seemed to be crowding in. Two of them came up to Arnie. 'C'mon, Mac, let's go.'

'Who's the officer in charge?' Arnie said.

The policeman's hand closed on his arm. Arnie's instinct was to shake it off, but he restrained himself. 'I'm a lawyer – I demand to speak to the officer in charge.' And he mentioned a couple of powerful names who worked out of the D.A.'s Office.

The officer sighed. 'Lieutenant Saxby – over there by the door.' He released Arnie's arm and let the other policeman guide him over to where the lieutenant stood.

He was a big brute of a man with a slab of broken nose and a complexion like mud. He was standing with his night-stick in one hand, smacking it into the palm of the other. Arnie did not recognise him at first, but there was something about that name . . . *Saxby*? . . . *SAXBY* . . . like a tiny voice trying to make itself heard in the wind.

Suddenly he remembered. The man had been with the L.A. Vice Squad, and Arnie had had the good luck to subpoena his wife as co-respondent in a divorce case he'd been handling a few years back. And when the covers were off, it turned out Mrs Saxby was a hooker. It didn't do her husband's reputation much good, nor did Arnie think Saxby would be in any hurry to embrace the instrument of his humiliation.

Arnie was not sure whether the lieutenant recognised him or not. It was sheer bravura that made him step up and say, 'Lieutenant Saxby, isn't it? Fancy meeting you here!'

For the moment the lieutenant was more interested in surveying the yards of naked flesh, like a hunter surveying his bag. Then slowly his piggy eyes shifted on to Arnie. 'Who the hell are you?'

'Arnold Becker – we crossed paths about four years back. I had your wife on the stand in the civil court.' He had to shout to make himself heard.

The man's mouth had sagged open. '*Becker?*'

'How you doing, Lieutenant? Still with the Vice Squad, I see.'

The man put his head back and roared, '*Can that music!*' He glowered at Arnie. 'You made out she was a lush. A whore.' The music suddenly stopped, and he lowered his voice. 'And you made out I was a drifter, a no-good. Said I was a wife-beater . . .' His breath was warm and rancid in Arnie's face.

Arnie smiled weakly. 'Well, you know how it is . . .'

'No, I don't know how it is. You tell me, *Mister* Becker.'

'I mean, I was only acting on instructions. As I remember it, the judge was pretty sympathetic towards you. Thought you were well shot of her. Which – for what it's worth – is rather what I felt too.'

'Yeah. Well it sure weren't the impression I got, Becker. Now move your butt.'

Two new policemen had suddenly appeared behind

Arnie and took hold of his arms. At that moment he caught a glimpse of Sally. He tried to call to her, but was swept outside by the two policemen. He found himself standing next to a middle-aged man wearing only Y-fronts and black socks, without shoes.

'What's going on?' Arnie asked.

'Police raid,' the man said thickly.

'I know that. But why?'

But before Arnie could listen to the answer, he was half pushed, half lifted into the police van, his tall frame squashed in with about a dozen other people. The air was hot and stank of perfume and aftershave. Arnie could hardly see anything. Someone was standing on his foot and his elbow seemed to be in another person's ribs, but he couldn't move.

'Will someone please tell me why we're here?' he pleaded into the darkness. The van started up and everyone lurched.

'They don't like us!' a voice said, with a shriek of laughter.

'We've been busted,' someone else explained, as though it were no more important than being held up in a traffic jam.

'Why? What's been going on?' asked Becker.

For some reason, everyone else in the van seemed to think this hilariously funny. Only Becker, it seemed, couldn't see the joke. He waited for the laughter to stop. And waited. And waited. At last someone near him – he wasn't certain if it was the person standing on his foot – gasped, in a tight androgenous voice, 'Didn't you go to the bathroom?'

'No.'

'You mean you didn't go into the little boys' room and smell something just a bit unusual?'

Arnie Becker remembered noticing the heady, nostalgic scent of marijuana when he was talking to Nina. Somehow it had seemed part of the whole scene. Still, hardly cause for a police raid of this size, he thought.

'Hey, we've got a straight guy here!' And they all collapsed with laughter again. Becker was getting uptight.

'Didn't you see the lines of coke in the john? Stretching from here to eternity. All done with mirrors. Or rather, on mirrors.'

Under a passing streetlight, he saw the man's face. Interchangeable with all the others: getting a little jowly, bags under the eyes, longish hair.

'Oh *no*!' Becker gasped. What an idiot he was! He had always thought of himself as so sophisticated: driving his swish red Mustang to the strains of Bob Dylan and Arlo Guthrie. And here he was, twenty years on, getting hooked into a party at the heart of Babylon, as streetwise as a newborn kitten.

'Yeah, Adrian was celebrating in style. Just got his twelfth gold disc – and all of them still in the charts. He's been growing marijuana on his sundeck – must have had at least twenty plants. Plus he keeps his stuff stashed away inside the flowerpots – reckons it's safe there. Poor guy – someone must have tipped off the police. Maybe that bimbo Lydia, the one he just pushed out. She was threatening a palimony suit.'

Becker wanted to bury his head in his hands but couldn't move his arms. Why had he succumbed to a last-minute phone call like a teenager? Why hadn't he stayed home and watched the movie?

The van screeched to a halt and the large unsmiling face of Lieutenant Saxby appeared in the doorway.

'OK you nerds. Outta here – and quick! You too, lawyer!' he added, flicking Becker painfully behind the knee, as he clambered out into the yard of the precinct house, glad that this ignominious journey was over. From the street outside came the panting scream of an ambulance siren.

*

There was an incredible hubbub of voices in the precinct house. As a divorce attorney, Becker rarely saw the seamier side of the law and a sight which would have been familiar to some of his colleagues struck him as overwhelming. Confusion reigned. There seemed to be no system at all.

Police officers kept bringing in more and more prisoners from the beach party. If they'd looked exotic there, they looked downright weird here under the stark overhead lighting of the bleak charge-room, like characters from a film where the director had got smashed and told the cast to dress and act just the way they liked. This was Hollywood, after all.

And because it was Hollywood, most people – police and prisoners alike – tended to treat everything as though it were more or less routine. The police jostled each other to get to the desk and book in their suspects. For a time their way was barred by an old lady with tears streaming down her face who was pounding on the desk with her handbag, wailing about her lost cat. Someone had brought in a stray parrot which every so often took off and flew around the crowded room, relieving itself on people's heads and shouting, 'I'm Napoleon Bonaparte!'

Arnie Becker sat on a bench with the other people from the party, some of whom looked quite familiar. Then he realised that at least half of them were faces he had frequently seen in the press and on posters.

Next to him he recognised a petite blonde girl who featured every Saturday night as a demure waitress in one of dimmer soaps on TV. She had gone to sleep sitting up, and one of her false eyelashes was missing. The other was insecurely gummed on, the mascara melting, and looked like a miniature iron railing.

Among the crush of other bleary, debauched faces he saw Nina, the psychic chiropodist. She had her dress back on, but it was wet and torn, although she appeared not to notice or care. She was kneading the big toe of the man sitting next to her. There was no sign of Sally.

Arnie thought regretfully of his unwatched video, his quiet evening at home. How far away it all seemed! He shifted his buttocks on the bench, trying hopelessly to find a comfortable position. He had almost become resigned to his state when Saxby reappeared. 'OK, you jerks. Follow me – and no funny business.'

The man had a great scriptwriter, Arnie thought; he should go into movies.

*

Arnie couldn't believe it when the cell door clanged shut behind him. This happened to other people – but how could it be happening to him? Arnie Becker, the successful divorce lawyer. Cool Arnie. Sophisticated Arnie. Successful Arnie. Not Incarcerated Arnie – that was all wrong.

Further indignity was to follow. They took his clothes away. He'd already given up his watch, his wallet and his credit cards. His Hermes tie had been roughly bundled into a brown envelope with his valuables. But now he was without jacket, shirt or pants. For what seemed like hours he cowered at the back of his cell, ashamed. He'd taken off his clothes in front of hundreds of girls but the thought of one of those tough policewomen seeing him in his underwear made him sweat.

At last they allowed him to dress again. Then they charged him with possessing cocaine.

'But how could I possess any? I didn't even know there were any drugs at the party!' Arnie blustered, and recognised something that he'd often heard about in the law: that the more preposterous the accusation, the more implausible sounds the denial.

The policeman held up a small plastic envelope containing a pinch of white powder, sealed within a larger plastic bag. 'This was found in the pocket of your pants,' he said.

'I've never seen that before!' Arnie cried, with genuine horror.

'Are you willing to sign a statement to that effect?'

'Certainly. It's the truth. It must have been planted.'

'That's a very serious allegation you're making,' growled the policeman.

'I can't imagine how else it got there,' Arnie said.

They wrangled back and forth. Eventually, they let Arnie go, with bail fixed at in his own cognisance, for five thousand dollars, on condition he appeared in court the next day. He stumbled out of the precinct house into the bright sunlight. Strapping his gold watch back on his wrist, he was horrified to realise it was 9am. Morning conference would be starting. Should he call in sick or go straight to the office?

3

McKenzie Hits
The Tiles

Leland McKenzie decided to go to his health club on the way home from the office around the time Arnie Becker had planned his quiet evening at home. Leland hadn't been feeling too good recently. His indigestion had got so bad that there was always a bottle of Pepto-bismol on his bedside table and he had cut down on rich food but that didn't seem to help. Nothing helped, least of all his doctor who just told him to take it easy and then presented him with a large bill. Maybe a work-out followed by a hot tub would get his juices going.

It felt good to pit his strength against the carefully balanced weight machines. The physical exertion made him feel much better and he was even able to forget about the office for a few minutes. His muscles seemed to hurt a lot but in a strange way the pain was soothing. The cold metal gleamed and he felt sweat first dripping, then pouring down his face, chest and back.

Leland stopped. When he first got off the machine, his legs would hardly take his weight. He felt dizzy and hot. Maybe he'd overdone it. His heart was pounding and he could feel the blood coursing through his veins. After a while, though, the room seemed to steady and he walked over to the bathing area.

He took a cold shower and then plunged into the hot tub. Two other men were already immersed, one of whom he had met several times in court. Leland was having trouble remembering his name, though, so he kept the conversation general. Complaining about his doctor was a good all-purpose subject.

'How can I take it easy?' he grumbled. 'I'm running that office, trying to keep everyone happy – I feel as

29

though I'm running a kindergarten sometimes – and trying to keep my clients happy, too.'

'Maybe you should think about taking early retirement, Leland,' said the man – Jim? John? Joe? Leland found he couldn't focus on his face or his name.

'Retire! How can I retire? I love that firm; I started it!' His face creased.

'Sure. But you must do as the doctor says. Take it easy. Otherwise you'll die at your desk like Norman Cheyney . . .'

'Don't say that!' The memory of his late partner's death, undiscovered for two days, was still bitter. Leland was surprised to feel an almost physical sensation of pain. The water suddenly seemed hotter. It was hard to breathe.

'I gotta get out of here,' he gasped.

The man he'd been talking to grabbed his arm but it was slippery with sweat. Leland collapsed under the water. He was vaguely aware of shouting, of hands clutching him. He was submerged in heat and darkness. Everything went black.

When he came to, he was lying uncomfortably by the side of the tub, his feet trailing in the water. Towels were draped over him and the masseur was manipulating his chest.

'Hey, that hurts!' Leland grunted.

The masseur smiled. 'Good,' he said. 'If it didn't hurt, I'd be real worried.'

Anxious faces swam into Leland's view. 'Are you all right?' asked the man he'd been talking to.

'No, I'm not all right. I feel awful, and I have this

terrible pain . . .' Leland clutched his left arm. 'And my chest hurts . . .' He was a dreadful ashen grey.

'The ambulance is on its way,' one of the faces said.

The faces went out of focus again and Leland lay back on the tiles. It was surprising how comfortable that hard floor felt . . .

They waited an anxious forty-five minutes. Leland floated in and out of consciousness, vaguely aware of the masseur pummelling his chest from time to time. At last the paramedics arrived and lifted him on to a stretcher. The ambulance driver looked terribly young, hardly more than a schoolboy, Leland thought, but his partner was a capable-looking woman.

Soon, Leland McKenzie was being wheeled into the emergency room at Bel Air Hospital, a mask over his face. Anxious paramedics surrounded him.

'Do you have medical insurance?' asked the nurse, holding her clipboard against her round bosom. She lifted his mask so that he could answer.

Leland turned to the girl. 'What kind of a question is that when a man is dying?'

'I'm sorry, sir, but I have to ask,' replied the nurse. 'I get into trouble if I don't. *Do* you have medical insurance?'

'Yes, I do. I'll give you all the details *after* I know that I'm being properly cared for,' Leland snapped. 'Now put that mask back on and go to hell.'

*

Morning conference. Douglas Brackman looked at his watch and tapped the table impatiently. Where *was* everybody? Only half the seats were taken. At least he could usually count on Leland to be punctual.

Roxanne hurried into the conference room, her face drawn. She came close to Brackman and spoke in a low voice. 'Bel Air Hospital has just been on the telephone. Mr McKenzie's in there – he's had a heart attack!'

Brackman's first reaction was one of irritation. How could Leland do this? First Stuart Markowitz and now . . . He drew a deep breath and composed himself.

'Oh, that's too bad. Is he still on the line?' he asked.

'No,' replied Roxanne. 'I didn't speak to him. A nurse rang. She apologised for not ringing sooner but it happened yesterday evening. Leland spent all night in Intensive Care. They didn't know whether he was going to make it.'

'How serious is it, then?' asked Brackman, becoming more concerned.

'It seems he'll live but they aren't able to tell whether he'll make a full recovery. They're keeping him in the hospital for observation and tests.' Roxanne looked near to tears.

Brackman stood up. Most of the places were filled now. 'People, I have an announcement to make. Our colleague Leland McKenzie has been taken ill. He has suffered a heart attack. All we know is that he's out of danger. We cannot tell if or when he will return to work.'

A babble of voices filled the room.

'We will have to spread his workload between us. Too bad he's just got a new secretary who doesn't know her way around. I know that his main problem at the moment is the Levine/Whittaker case. I'll take that on myself. Also, for today, I will deal with his mail and telephone calls. Tomorrow morning I will bring a full list of his cases to the conference and –'

He broke off as Arnold Becker entered the room.

'Good evening, Arnie,' he said, with grim sarcasm. 'What have we done to deserve the pleasure of your company at this late hour?'

Becker knew the moment he walked in that he looked awful. While last night he'd been the best dressed prisoner at the precinct house, here at the morning conference at McKenzie Brackman he was not only the worst dressed, he looked crushed and ill: his face wan, hair dishevelled, dark mushrooms under the eyes. His only concession to respectability was to have borrowed the electric shaver from the janitor in the basement. But the most damning evidence was his suit which looked as though he'd slept in it – which he had. Roxanne, ever protective, hurried to his side. He fumbled for words.

'I'm real sorry, I . . . er . . . got delayed.'

Douglas Brackman showed great irritation at this obvious statement.

'Well, now you're here you had better catch up on the bad news. Leland's in hospital with a heart attack. As I was saying, we'll all have to share his workload and we'll decide tomorrow morning who will do what. Meanwhile, Arnold, perhaps – if you can spare the time – you would like to divulge your plans for the Gloria Gonzales divorce case.'

Becker looked blank, then embarrassed.

'I'm sorry,' he repeated. 'It's been . . . er . . . driven from my mind.'

33

'That *will* make a good impression on Mrs Gonzales at your meeting with her today,' sneered Brackman. 'Have you taken on a more important client since we last spoke? Is that why you're so late?'

Becker, who had been hoping for a quiet word with McKenzie about the beach party business, realised that he would have to come clean in front of all his colleagues.

'Something very unfortunate happened last night,' he began . . .

4

A Case of Verbal Assault

The faces round the conference table seemed to blur and recede as Arnie Becker spoke. After his first few stumbling words he gained confidence. It was almost as though he was talking about someone else – a client, maybe.

'. . . So I had no idea what had been going on until the guy in the police van told me. At the precinct house they didn't believe me at first when I said who I was. Then they threw me in a cell anyway. I didn't get any sleep – all those other people were still high. They talked and shouted to each other all night. And a lot of other people were brought in after us – muggers and thieves. It was so uncomfortable, too. And the smell . . .'

'You'll have to think of it as a learning experience, Arnie,' said Ann Kelsey brightly. 'It will give you more understanding if you're ever dealing with suspects.'

'Gee, thanks,' muttered Becker. 'I needed a learning experience like a hole in the head.'

Douglas Brackman frowned. 'You're sure you didn't touch any of the drugs, Becker?'

'Sure.'

'Did the police check your clothing?'

'Yeah, they took away my jacket, shirt and pants.' Becker shivered at the memory of sitting in his cell wearing nothing but socks and shorts.

'Did they find anything?' Brackman asked aggressively. 'Someone at the party might have planted some drugs. Even the police have been known to –'

'That's just it. I didn't have anything – didn't even know there were drugs at the party – but the police say they found some cocaine in the pocket of my pants. I have to appear in court tomorrow. It was lucky they let me out on bail this morning. At first they were going to keep me in till the hearing.'

The full impact of the situation crystallised in Arnie's mind as he spoke. He might go to jail for something he hadn't done! There was no way of proving his innocence. He'd never been on the wrong side of the law before.

'Right,' said Brackman. 'I believe you. We'll stand by you and . . . let's see . . . Victor will represent you in court. OK, Victor? Arnie? But we mustn't tell Leland. Not in his condition – it would finish him off.'

'Absolutely!' said Markowitz with feeling.

'Now,' Brackman continued, 'what are we going to do about Gloria Gonzales? If she finds out her attorney is up on a drugs charge, all hell will break loose. You know how puritanical she is – and how good she is at getting publicity too.'

'That's right,' said Mike Kuzak. 'There's already been a lot of coverage about her impending divorce. She mentioned Arnie and McKenzie Brackman in all her interviews – said how glad she was to have such an upright, reliable firm on her side.'

'Well, we *are* an upright, reliable firm,' said Stuart Markowitz. 'Just because one of our number gets taken to a party by a girl he hardly knows, given by a guy he's never met, who happens to be some kind of dopehead . . . that doesn't mean the partnership is a hotbed of vice.'

'Sure, but that's how we look at it. Gloria Gonzales may see it quite differently – meaning how will the publicity affect her ratings.' Victor Sifuentes spoke vehemently. 'She's brilliant at twisting the truth to suit herself. Look how she can switch from one point of view to another in midstream during her show and take the studio audience with her – and her millions of viewers, too.'

'Her latest campaign is a drugs hotline for school-kids,' said Abby. 'Did you see her show on Tuesday? She's about to open a switchboard which kids can call if they're on drugs and need help. And she's encouraging them to call even if they are just offered drugs. You know how all these pushers are hanging around outside schools.'

'Very commendable,' said Brackman drily. 'Just extremely bad timing from our point of view.'

The faces of Arnie Becker's colleagues swam before him. He leaned forward against the table, feeling a damp film of sweat breaking out on his brow. 'Excuse me,' he said, and ran from the room.

*

The meeting broke up; it was getting late and the telephones were buzzing with anxious clients seeking reassurance from their attorneys. Abby often felt that she should have trained as a psychiatrist rather than as a lawyer.

Some of McKenzie Brackman's clients seemed to be compulsive litigants – like Abby's first case of the day: an action brought by a certain Count Yevgeny Oblomov, a Russian.

Abby wasn't sure she'd ever met a Russian before – and certainly not a Count, for that matter. Although this was to be her first encounter with him, the file on her desk was already several inches thick. It contained copies of previous litigations, a number of which were against other law firms which had formerly represented him.

Leland McKenzie had taken on this man as a favour to an old friend and had immediately passed the case to Abby with the wry comment: 'If this doesn't put you off the legal profession, nothing will.' Abby had been counting on Leland's support and advice, particularly regarding this initial meeting, so his sudden illness had thrown her completely. She felt as though she was about to take an examination for which she hadn't revised.

When the intercom buzzed and the Count was announced, she could feel her heart hammering against her ribs, her mouth dry with anticipation and dread.

There was a loud rap on the door; she called out, 'Come in!' in a hoarse whisper; and a very tall, shambling, badly-dressed figure shuffled into the room and deposited two brown bags on the floor beside the door.

Abby wasn't quite sure what she'd expected, except that the idea of a Russian Count suggested something vaguely virile and glamorous, in the Ronald Colman line. She now found herself wondering whether Count Oblomov would manage to get as far as her visitor's chair.

He was deathly pale, with that papery-grey pallor of a new corpse; and besides being very tall, he was far too thin for his height. He wore a shapeless corduroy suit of indeterminate colour, what looked like an army tunic, a flashy gold wristwatch and a pair of brogue shoes, one of which had the laces missing.

'Good morning, my dear!' He fixed her with leaky eyes, and suddenly gave her a wolfish yellow smile. She guessed, instinctively, that he'd once been a ladies' man – was *still* a ladies' man, if anyone gave him the chance.

Nervously, she glanced at the bulging file. She had read it several times but still found it hard to follow. Then she remembered a ploy which Ann Kelsey had mentioned to her.

'Please would you tell me in your own words . . . er . . . Count Oblomov . . . exactly why you intend to bring an action against Mr Shaw?'

'Why? Why? Because he is a criminal! He has assaulted me!' For such a frail man, his voice was surprisingly loud and his eyes bulged alarmingly.

'But . . . er . . . I understand that Mr Shaw is bringing a counter-suit against *you* for assaulting him.'

'That is correct,' said the Russian.

'Did you assault him?' asked Abby hesitantly.

'Yes, of course I did. In self-defence.'

'What happened exactly?'

'We were having argument. About what, you might ask? About a verb!'

Abby gulped. 'Excuse me, I didn't quite hear . . .'

'Verb. Verrrrb. "To go". In Russian there are more than twenty ways of saying "to go". That idiot Shaw does not understand. He claims to know Russian. Ha!' The Count's eyes again bulged dangerously.

'We were collaborating on a movie. I am writing script about double agent escaping over the Berlin Wall. Already the Berlin Wall is nostalgia. For a while the Cold War was out of favour as a subject – now it is becoming fashionable again.'

Suddenly a bell clanged in the region of the Russian's left hip. He removed from his pocket an old-fashioned alarm clock which he thumped, silencing it; then took out a tiny enamel box, opened it and swallowed something from inside. 'Excusing me, please,' he said to Abby. 'I must take medicine for my gout.'

Abby wondered whether she had fallen asleep and was having a nightmare.

Having swallowed his pill, Count Oblomov continued. 'The studio says my English is not good enough and I must work with this Shaw. He is so insensitive. He does not understand nuances of Russian language which must be transported to the audience. All he knows is pace and action – nothing of *feeeeeling*.' He glared at Abby.

'I think I understand,' she said, almost truthfully.

'I am sure you do not, but at least you try. Shaw does not try to understand. All he tries is my patience.' He did not seem to notice that he'd made a mild pun. 'So in the end, my patience is finished and – *biff* – we fight!'

'He claims that you attacked him first.'

'I did not attack him. I offered him flowers – red roses.'

'Offered? I understood you threw a vase at his head.'

'It slipped from out of my hand. He was sitting at the desk. I was holding the vase. Suddenly, roses and water all over desk . . . and Shaw.'

'And the vase?'

'Yes, that was unfortunate. It made a large bruise.

42

But then he sprang up and grabbed me. My nose was broken – you see?'

The Count turned his profile to Abby who saw that his nose was indeed a strange shape. She also took the opportunity to glance at her watch.

'My goodness, is that the time!' she exclaimed. 'Unfortunately, I have another meeting. *So* good of you to come and see me, Count. I'll be in touch as soon as I've had a chance to consider your case.'

The Russian stood up, gaping at her. 'That is everything?'

'For the time being,' she said, with a brave smile. She watched him pick up the bags by the door and shuffle outside; then she tottered to her chair and collapsed in a heap. She didn't know whether to laugh or cry.

5

Up on Rodeo Drive

Roxanne was distraught. She didn't know whether to be more upset by Leland McKenzie's sudden illness or her precious Arnie's wrongful arrest. Like a mother hen, she overwhelmed him with zealous care and many strong cups of black coffee – her recent campaign against caffeine being momentarily forgotten.

Otherwise, the office seemed to be ticking over more or less normally. The two receptionists – dizzy-looking blondes called Candice and Jayne – spent most of the day giggling on the telephone, comparing fashion notes, or, if things were really quiet, doing their nails.

Arnie Becker spent a long time closeted in his office with Douglas Brackman and Victor Sifuentes. They were going over the previous night's events. As he was so tired, Arnie found it difficult to piece together a coherent picture of what had happened.

'Didn't you wonder why everyone kept going indoors?' Victor asked him.

'Well . . . yes. But I just thought they were going to the john. Which they were, but not for the usual reason.'

'And this girl Sally – was she arrested?' Victor persisted.

'No, I didn't see her afterwards. But Nina was at the precinct house.'

'Nina?'

'A girl who told me she was a psychic chiropodist, just before the raid began.'

'She said she was *what*?' Douglas snorted. 'A *psychic chiropodist*? You must have suspected something when she said that.'

'It didn't seem suspicious then, just unusual,' replied

Arnie. 'Anyway, maybe that's how she does earn her living. People go to chiropodists and they have their fortunes told. Maybe doing both simultaneously saves time if they're busy.'

Brackman gave him an old-fashioned look and continued. 'Now, it seems most likely to me that the drugs were planted on you in the police van. Or did the police take away your clothing before you were driven to the precinct house?'

Becker shook his head.

'You're right!' Victor exclaimed. 'All of you crammed in there together like you said. One of the other detainees could easily have dropped the cocaine into your pocket. But how can we prove it in court?'

'And, more to the point, how can we prove it to Ms Gonzales?' Brackman grunted. 'If she takes her divorce case away from us there'll be a big splash in the press and on television, make no mistake. And she won't hold back on saying why.'

'She did a programme last month on the subject of punishment for drug pushers,' Victor said. 'She thinks they're getting off much too lightly. Her studio audience were right behind her. Some of them wanted the death penalty! And she had this politician on the show who wants to cut off drug pushers' fingers.'

Arnie blenched. His stomach wasn't up to this. 'What can we do?' he asked despairingly. 'If we tell her the truth she won't believe it. If we cover up, she's bound to find out. It's a vicious circle and there's no way out.'

*

Later, Ann Kelsey went to the ladies' room where she found Abby trying to restore her composure and her make-up.

'So many legal actions are unnecessary, don't you think?' Abby asked Ann after she had told her about the Count.

'You're right,' Ann replied. 'People go to law in a spirit of revenge. Money won in damages can't right a wrong. Nobody benefits except lawyers. Still, that's what we're here for.' She combed her hair and applied more lipstick.

Abby sighed. 'I guess so.'

'Sounds like you've had a hard morning,' said Ann sympathetically. 'I know – why don't we take a long lunch hour and go shopping? I could do with some new clothes. Don't tell anyone else, though. Shopping always seems like such a frivolous thing to do.'

Abby checked her diary. 'I should really spend some more time studying the Count's life but I don't have another meeting till 4. What a great idea! We need cheering up after the sad news about Leland. How is he, by the way?'

'The hospital called again,' Ann said. 'No change in his condition, but he's quite comfortable. Douglas is going to see him this afternoon.'

A few minutes later, Ann and Abby slipped out of the office and found a taxi.

'Rodeo Drive, please,' Ann said to the driver.

'Wow! Are you in the money?' exclaimed Abby.

'No, but there might be some clothes at reduced prices and, anyway, it's fun to look around there,' Ann said. 'You know what they say: when the going gets tough, the tough go shopping.'

'Did anyone see us leave the office?' asked Abby.

'I think maybe Roxanne did,' Ann replied. 'She has eyes in the back of her head. Never mind. Oh, isn't this *fun*! I feel as though we're playing hookey from school.'

They spent a happy hour wandering in and out of shops. Ann bought an outrageous tracksuit covered with hand-painted strawberries and fake rubies. Abby was more strong-minded but indulged in a pair of tennis socks. One was embroidered with the words *I'm gonna win* and the other *You're gonna lose*.

'And I meant to buy a sober business suit to wear in court!' said Ann happily as they emerged from the elevator. She quickly hid her large bag in the ladies' room so nobody would find out about their secret jaunt. As luck would have it, the two women came under Douglas Brackman's stern gaze as they sneaked into the office.

*

At a large house near Rodeo Drive the curtains were drawn despite the bright sun. Grilles barred the windows. A security camera surveyed the front gate which was made of solid metal, set in a high wall topped with spikes. Other cameras were aimed so as to give complete coverage of the property. The garden was immaculate but uninviting. Who could wander there, carelessly admiring the shrubs and smelling the flowers, under the cameras' glare?

A side door opened and quickly closed. A man wearing a large panama hat pulled over his brow, his eyes disguised by large black sunglasses, slipped into the house and hurried unobtrusively along the richly-carpeted corridor. The door he was looking for stood ajar.

The room he entered was a dream – or nightmare. Every artifice of the latest fashion in interior decor had been incorporated into the design. The drawn curtains were but a small part of the layers of ruched blinds, pelmets, swags and valances which surrounded the windows. These were echoed in the drapes of the massive four-poster bed.

Lying on the bed was a woman, draped almost as excessively as the windows, in a flounced silk and lace *negligee*. The man silently moved towards her. Her body quivered sensuously in anticipation.

6

Queen of the
Small Screen

Arnie Becker had a jacuzzi and sauna in place of lunch. He fell asleep in the pine-lined room for half an hour and woke dry-mouthed, streaming with sweat. A cold plunge, followed by a Virgin Mary with lots of tabasco sauce, revived him sufficiently to confront Gloria Gonzales although his brain still seemed to be working at half speed.

She swept into his office preceded by the heady scent of *Giorgio*. Her well-cut dress – bright yellow to contrast with her smooth tan and dark hair – was immaculate and she flashed her famous smile at Arnie. On television, she seemed to have double the usual number of teeth and their number did not diminish in real life.

Becker was surprised, however, to find that she was quite small despite her overwhelming personality – which was just as electric off screen as on. She gazed up at him while they shook hands, as though to accentuate their difference in height, and for a moment made herself appear vulnerable. Suddenly, he felt an urge to protect her.

'Oh, Mr Becker,' she murmured. 'I'm so glad you are going to look after me.'

Having been prepared to dislike her, especially in the circumstances of his arrest, he now found himself hypnotised by Gloria Gonzales. However, a niggling instinct at the back of his mind warned him to be wary of her charm.

'You cannot imagine, Mr Becker, what it is like to have to be brave in front of millions of viewers when inside I want to weep.' Her face portrayed despair.

'It makes me feel such a fool,' she continued. 'For years I have encouraged couples to be faithful, to abide by their marriage vows, to stay together through thick and thin. I have campaigned to make it more difficult to get divorced – and more difficult to get married in the first place. Marriage is treated so lightly these days . . .'

She turned as though to face another camera, then switched her full gaze back on Arnie. '. . . And now I must go through this humiliating process myself. But I will not . . . cannot . . . continue to live under the same roof as this man who has betrayed me.'

'I quite understand,' murmured Arnie, in his best honeyed tone. 'We will make it as easy as possible for you.'

'You see,' Gloria Gonzales said. 'It isn't only the betrayal that hurts. It's the deception. I can't tolerate deception.'

Arnie felt his stomach muscles clench involuntarily.

'Of course, Mrs Gonzales, of course.'

'Oh!' she opened her eyes very wide. 'Please call me Gloria. Gonzales is my own name. I rarely use *his* name. I will never do so again.'

'What is his name, for the record?'

A pause. Then she whispered, 'Morton Smellie.'

*

Douglas Brackman was stuck in a traffic jam – one of the joys of living in Los Angeles. He was on his way to visit Leland McKenzie in hospital. At last the cars started moving; then the one in front of him stalled. It was being driven by a grey-haired lady who could hardly see over the steering wheel. He pulled over and got out.

'May I help you, ma'am?' he asked, through gritted teeth.

'Why, thank you. How unusual to find such politeness in this city,' she replied, in a thick Central European accent. She sounded like a stage psychiatrist. Trustingly, she moved over so that Brackman could slide into the driver's seat.

He tested the ignition. The engine wheezed and coughed. Once. Twice. Nothing. However, the radio came on briefly and he half heard the newsreader say: '. . . *at his Malibu home. Several arrests were made and charges will be brought tomorrow. And now the weather in the Los Angeles area . . .*'

He was about to risk getting oil on his hands by opening the hood when his eye caught the fuel gauge. Empty. Meanwhile, behind them, an orchestra of angry horns were blaring at them both, as the drivers counted up the lost seconds of their lives.

Brackman said, in a deep tone of authority, 'Ma'am, you have run out of gas. That is why your car won't start.'

'You know, my son is always telling me I will run out of gas but I never have done so before. Maybe that is because he takes the car to the gas station every week and fills it up. But this week he is in Florida on business.'

The words flowed on relentlessly, as thick as clotted Viennese *Schlagzahnne*; and Brackman, from long experience of dealing with little old ladies, knew that if he didn't escape now, he would have to hear her entire life story. He opened the car door and leapt out, then yelled through the window, 'When I get where I'm going, I'll call an emergency tow truck to come find you. Meanwhile, sit tight and don't let anyone in the car.'

'But I let *you* in!'

'Yes, but it so happens I'm not a murderer or a rapist. I'm an attorney. Now, *take care*.' Automatically, he extracted his business card from his wallet and gave it to her.

Seething, he returned to his car, manoeuvred the wheel skilfully, and arrived at the hospital without further interruptions.

*

Leland was propped up on pillows, his bare chest dotted with electrodes. Green screens flashed and blipped behind his bed which was piled with books and newspapers. A nurse was fussing over him.

'I'll leave you two alone,' said the nurse officiously. 'But promise not to tire him. No more than ten minutes, mind.' She left the room.

'So, how are things back at the ranch?' asked Leland.

'Busy. OK. Everyone was very shocked by the news but they're all prepared to put in extra time. So don't worry about your work.'

'I can't help worrying. They tell me it's worry that caused this damned heart attack. That fool of a doctor kept telling me to take it easy. Easy! Maybe his life is easy but mine isn't.'

The lines on the screens became more jagged and the blips grew louder.

'Listen, Leland,' said Douglas. 'Look what happened to Markowitz. He survived. But let's face it, he's much younger than you. I know I've been giving him a hard time since he returned to the office but somehow I feel he hasn't much backbone and I need to keep him on his toes.'

Leland nodded.

'But you've literally put your heart and soul into the firm,' Brackman continued. 'And it's time for you to relax a little. Let it ride for a while. We've got a good team.'

'Are you sure?' Leland asked wrily.

'Yeah, sure.'

'No weak links in the chain?'

'None.'

'What about Arnie Becker, then?'

Although he was normally in full control of himself, Douglas Brackman was taken unawares and he gaped at his partner.

'Well, is it true?' Leland persisted.

'Is what true?'

'Oh, come on. Don't fool with me. This drugs business.'

Douglas got a grip on himself. 'Becker swears he was set up. He knew nothing about drugs at the party until he was on his way to the precinct house. Someone must have planted some dope on him – maybe even the police. But, Leland, how did you know about it? Nobody knows outside the office.'

'That's what you think,' said McKenzie wrily. 'I guess you've been too busy to read the small print in the newspapers.'

59

He foraged in the pile of papers on his bed and pulled out the *L.A. Clarion*. On Page 3 was a headline:

ROCK STARS' DRUG BUST COOLS LUST

The ensuing story concentrated on the chart-topping personalities who had been among the guests at the party given by 'award-winning record producer Adrian Calvados'. According to the colourful report, they had been about to embark on a gargantuan orgy when the raid happened.

At the foot of the page, in tiny print, was a full list of those arrested. Only three rock stars had been grabbed by the police. The rest – as far as most of the *Clarion*'s readers were concerned – were nonentities.

'How did you spot Arnie's name?' asked Douglas.

'I was testing my new bifocals,' Leland replied. 'I just got them yesterday. Hadn't been able to read print that size for quite a while.'

'Well, let's hope Gloria Gonzales is too vain to wear spectacles or doesn't have time to read all the papers,' Brackman said.

Leland shook his head. 'You'll have to come clean with her. Otherwise she'll find out anyway and that will be even worse.'

The nurse bustled back into the room, looked horrified at the configurations on the screens, and shooed Brackman out. He remembered that he hadn't called a tow truck for the old lady and, despite an urge to leave her stranded, went to find a telephone.

7

Vodka . . . Ice-Cold in L.A.

Ann Kelsey kicked off her shoes and started to make supper for herself. Stuart had warned her he would be late back as he had to see a client after hours. While she absent-mindedly prepared a salad, she worried that he was working too hard. He often had to stay late these days.

'If only Douglas would quit needling him!' she thought. 'Can't he see that this pressure is the worst thing for him?'

But she knew that any attempt to slow down her husband would be met with irritation at best and anger at worst – and that, too, would do no good. She just had to let go.

Matthew gave her a beaming smile. She picked him up and hugged him tight. Sometimes it felt good to stop being an attorney and become a mother.

Matthew was fast asleep and Ann had bathed, washed her hair, and even found time to paint her toenails by the time Stuart came home. She was reading some files when he walked in.

'What would you like to eat, honey?'

'Don't worry about me,' he replied. 'I picked up a snack on the way home. Don't forget, I'm trying to lose weight.' He flopped into an armchair and opened his briefcase.

Ann was tempted to say something about not working too hard. They both sat, studying their papers and listening to music companionably, for about an hour. Ann noticed that Stuart couldn't seem to relax but she became so absorbed in her notes – another case about a medical insurance company

63

that wouldn't pay up – that she soon forgot his tension.

*

Count Oblomov took his last bottle of Stolichnaya vodka out of the deep freeze. It was so cold that it stuck to his fingers and he remembered the time when his hand and lips were burnt by touching such an icy bottle as this. He had heard of a man who had died from drinking ice-cold vodka – the skin of his throat burned raw, as though by fire.

It was thoughts like this that made the Count wonder whether life were really worth living. As usual he decided that it probably wasn't, but that he did not want the end to come quite yet.

He hardly ever ate now. The taste and sight of hamburgers, club sandwiches and other fast food disgusted him; but as usual, that was all he could afford. He longed for *blinis* with caviar; exquisite dishes of salmon wrapped in paper-thin pastry; great hunks of *filet mignon* . . . In fact, he had never been able to afford such luxuries, although he lived in a state of grace in which he imagined this to have been his regular diet in a luxurious past which had not really existed.

Oblomov had left Russia in the fifties, while serving as a military intelligence officer with the Soviet occupying forces in Vienna. For a time the Americans thought him to be a prize source of information; but Oblomov soon quarrelled with his benefactors and, after drifting round the capitals of Western Europe, he set off for America to seek his fortune.

Besides Russian he knew a number of languages, none of them well, but enough to be able to scratch a living as a translator. He also found work with radio stations and specialist publications, wearily trawling through hours of broadcasts from the Soviet Union in the hope of picking up some nugget of valuable information. Sometimes he translated books, but invariably ended up having a bitter quarrel with the publisher or collaborator, or both.

At other times he had tried his hand as a freelance journalist, but laboured under the misapprehension that any attempt to cut or prune his work was somehow a slur on his manhood. And since he wrote at colossal length, he soon found his outlets silting up.

However, he saw all these tasks as temporary and insignificant ways of making money. One day he would be rich – really rich. Oblomov was a gambler. Formerly he had gambled at roulette tables, poker games, back-gammon boards and racecourses. On the rare occasions when he won, he either spent his winnings in a splurge of giddy generosity, or would immediately play again, until he'd lost everything – and sometimes more than everything. Friends – usually his compatriots – lent him money knowing they would never be repaid.

Eventually he ran out of friends. Then, seeing head-lines in the newspapers about the huge sums being awarded in damages by the U.S. courts, he quite simply embarked on a career of litigation.

Because he was both persistent and annoying, the actions he initiated were frequently settled out of court, in order to prevent an expensive and exhausting trial. In this way he would be awarded relatively small sums, tax-free, which would have gone some way to cover his living expenses – if he hadn't spent the lot either celebrating or gambling.

'But this time,' he thought, as he sipped the vodka, 'this time I will win a fortune. Maybe I will sue the film company, as well as Shaw.' It was only a small film company, operating on a shoestring, and Oblomov and his collaborator were lucky to have been paid anything. But to Oblomov a Hollywood film company was like the bottomless mines of El Dorado . . .

He had forgotten that the chance to write a script had come as a favour from one of his few remaining friends, an independent producer whose last movie had been a worthy flop.

*

Arnie Becker and Victor Sifuentes stayed late in the office, working out what to say at the hearing the next day.

'The problem is that your innocence – your ignorance of what was happening – just doesn't sound plausible,' said Victor. 'I know it's true because I know you and believe in you. You're a real innocent in some ways.'

It was years since Becker had been called innocent. He raised his eyebrows.

'Any streetwise kid of twelve or even younger could have guessed what was going on,' Victor continued. 'But here we are, in our ivory tower. We only see the real world as it chooses to come to us. Sure, we deal with drugs cases but it's the seamy aspect of drugs we're familiar with, not the social side.'

'The social side – what happened last night – is probably just as dangerous,' Arnie said. 'The fact I didn't realise what was happening made it worse in some ways. More insidious. I must say, Gloria has a point.'

'Yes, Gloria Gonzales. What *are* we going to say to her?' As Victor spoke, the telephone rang. He picked it up.

'I'll see if he's available, Ms Gonzales. One moment, please. I'll just put you on hold.'

He put his free hand over his eyes and held out the receiver. Arnie took a deep breath. 'Can't you say I'll call her back?'

'No, Arnie. The longer you leave it, the worst it will get. You must talk to her *now*. I've got a feeling she already knows. She sounded pretty angry.'

'But how can she know?'

Victor put the receiver into his hand. 'Ask her.'

'Hello, Gloria.' Arnie put on his smoothest voice. From where she was sitting, Victor could hear a volley of words coming out of the receiver. Occasionally, Arnie managed to contribute a word but the conversation was largely one-sided. When Gloria finished talking, she slammed down the telephone.

Becker's tall frame crumpled in his chair. 'Come on, Arnie. Don't give in now,' Victor said. 'Listen, you must be starving. Let's go eat.'

'Haven't you got a date?' Becker asked.

'Nothing doing,' said Victor. 'I've been spending some pretty quiet evenings recently.'

They went to a small Italian trattoria in Santa Monica where they could talk quietly. Over a steaming plate of lasagne, Becker said, 'Maybe I should write to Gloria

67

as she won't listen to me. The irony is, she did a pro-gramme about a year ago on injustice, wrongful impris-onment, fabricated evidence – that kind of thing. Maybe I can remind her of it and persuade her to believe me.'

'That's a great idea, Arnie,' Victor said. 'Let's draft it now – then Roxanne can type it up first thing and send it by messenger.'

8

Kind Hearts And Kleenex

A special late afternoon conference had been called at McKenzie Brackman so that Arnie's colleagues could hear about the court hearing which had begun that morning.

'I've never seen anything like it,' said Victor. 'It was standing room only. The people who couldn't get in were so angry that the court officials had to rig up a sound system with loudspeakers in another room. There were fans, press, bodyguards . . .'

'And how did you get on, Arnie?' Douglas Brackman asked.

'Not too bad,' Arnie replied. 'The newshounds weren't interested in me. Most of the other defendants are household names – but who's heard of Arnie Becker? Normally I'd mind. But in the circumstances . . . Anyway, when the story broke about Andromeda Fulton, even the other rock stars were eclipsed.'

'Andromeda *who*? What story?'

'She's that Lolita-type kid – says she's thirteen but looks eighteen going on thirty-five. Her hit record is on every radio station. Even you must have heard it, Doug? *Low Fat, High Protein*, it's called. Very suggestive. She's even sexier than Madonna – so they say. Though not my type.'

'Get back on the subject, Becker,' said Brackman.

'The point is, Andromeda was at the party. Looked just like all the other girls – skirt up to here and legs like spaghetti – but like I said, it seems she really *is* only thirteen. She's accused of being involved in the drugs business. And Adrian Calvados, the guy whose party it was, is accused of having sex with her on the

71

beach. That was sparked off by the *Clarion* story. Their chief reporter claims he saw them.'

'Wow,' said Mike Kuzak. 'That's serious stuff. It could finish his career – it's happened to better people before.'

'It's hard to believe she *is* only thirteen,' said Victor. 'If she looks like that now, what's she going to look like when she's thirty? And what's left for her to do?'

'I think it's wicked!' exclaimed Ann Kelsey. 'I don't know how any mother could allow her child to behave like that. Have you seen Andromeda on TV? Her performance is horrendous. It makes me sick. And they say her mother actually encourages her.' Her eyes filled with tears.

'Are you feeling all right, Ann?' asked Abby.

'No, I'm not,' she snapped.

'Mrs Kelsey, please control yourself,' said Douglas. 'And for heaven's sake, let's get back on track.' Ann Kelsey shot him a look of pure hatred, gathered up her papers and left the room.

Brackman appeared not to notice, and said, 'OK, Arnold, what's next in the court procedure?'

'They couldn't get through all the business today. It was chaos. I haven't been called yet.'

'And how are you going to plead?' Brackman raised an eyebrow and fixed Becker with a stare. As so often before, he reminded Becker of a hawk about to pounce.

'Not guilty, of course.'

'Like I said before, Arnold, we'll stand by you. But you must tell the whole truth.'

Becker blustered, 'But I told you the truth. If I can't

make you believe what I say, what chance have I in court?'

'Have you ever taken drugs?' Brackman quizzed him.

'In college. Like everyone did. Nothing since, I swear.' Becker's suave appearance, restored for the court hearing, began to crumple. Even his suit looked tired.

'OK. Let's hope there's no police record of your carefree college days.'

*

Ann Kelsey fled to the ladies' room and dissolved in tears, holding on to the washbasin. 'That foul, awful man,' she sobbed. 'I hate him, I hate him.' Having started to cry, all her other woes rose to the surface and the tears came flooding out. The door swung open. It was Roxanne.

'Listen, honey, don't you take any notice of him. You know, I sometimes wonder whether he's human. He certainly doesn't have any feelings.'

Ann tried to stop crying, caught sight of her red nose in the mirror, and started again.

'I'll get you a cup of tea,' said Roxanne and bustled out. Left alone, Ann sank on to a chair and allowed herself to think about the real reason why she was so upset.

That woman. The one Stuart had taken to lunch. He'd been very odd about it; hadn't mentioned that he had a lunch date. Said he was busy when Ann suggested a swim at the health club in their lunch break. Then, on her way back to the office after swimming alone, she saw them. Stuart was helping the woman into a taxi. Being charming. Kissing her hand. The memory made Ann feel sick.

Then Roxanne hurried in with a cup of tea. 'Here you are, dear. I expect you have low blood sugar. I made you herb tea and here's a muesli bar.' If Ann hadn't been feeling so low, she would have teased Roxanne about being back on her health kick.

'Thanks, Roxanne, that's real kind of you.' She took a sip. 'Tell me, I know you don't work for Stuart but did you happen to see his diary today? I can't remember the name of the woman he had lunch with but I'm sure I recognised her.'

'Why yes. That was Mrs Emily Stallwood. Did you see her? Isn't she lovely?'

Ann gritted her teeth and nodded.

Roxanne continued. 'I didn't realise you knew her. She's an old friend of Stuart's; he handled her affairs for a while and she used to come in quite often. She married a very rich man – rich even by West Coast standards, so I heard. Marcus, I think his first name is. He's still quite young, and nobody really knows where his money comes from. One story has it that he inherited a family fortune and they both moved to Europe. Was it Switzerland? Anyway, they're back now. I believe Stuart is doing some work for Mrs Stallwood . . .'

While Roxanne rambled on, tears continued to well in Ann's eyes. Roxanne was telling her far more than she wanted to know.

Seeing the tears, Roxanne proffered a Kleenex. 'Don't take on so about Douglas, he's not worth it.'

Ann had almost forgotten about her scrap with Brackman. She stood up. 'Thanks, Roxanne. I'm OK now. I think I'll go home and make an early start tomorrow.'

*

This time, they met in a small hotel outside the city, off Highway 1. They arrived in separate cars. He got there first and collected the keys at the desk. Their cabin was some distance from the main building.

From outside, it looked very simple. The walls were of rough-hewn logs still covered in bark. The roof was made of wood shingles. Inside, an air of quiet luxury reigned. The room was decorated in muted earth colours. Everything was soft and sensuous. An open fireplace laid with logs of juniper and mesquite filled the room with a delicious dry scent. On the table was a tray of tropical fruit and a bottle of champagne in a cooler.

Soon the door opened and she slipped in, wearing wraparound sunglasses and a large straw hat which completely hid her hair.

'Did anyone see you arrive?' he asked.

'No. Maybe just a gardener. But I came straight to the cabin. We haven't much time, I'll have to get back.'

'OK. Let's go.' With one swift movement, he undid her heavy silk dress and it dropped to the floor. She was still wearing her hat as he pulled her down on top of him.

*

Again, Douglas Brackman fought the heavy afternoon traffic to the hospital. Why had McKenzie chosen this inconvenient time to summon him? Normally, Brackman answered to nobody – but the firm's senior partner, who was quite possibly on his deathbed, had to be an exception.

At last, he arrived at the hospital.

'I guess you want to know how the hearing went today.'

'Sure I do,' said Leland McKenzie, making an effort to ignore the electrodes on his chest. He felt so humiliated lying there half-naked while his partner loomed over him in a business suit. 'Oh, for heaven's sake, sit down!'

Douglas Brackman began recounting what had been said at the afternoon conference, but Leland interrupted him.

'That can wait. Sure, it's important, but wait till you hear this. Igor Strauss came to see me today. You know, the old guy who used to be with Radcliffes, Noach and Williams. He'd heard some gossip, and I've been lying here thinking about what he said. Each time I think about it, that damp blip goes off the screen. They keep telling me to calm down. Next thing, they'll say no visitors.'

'What did he say, Leland?' Douglas was trying to keep his patience.

McKenzie spoke in a deliberately controlled voice, pausing between each word. 'He said that another law firm – he couldn't or wouldn't say which – was trying to head-hunt two of our people. But he couldn't tell me who. So where does that leave us? I'm out of action for goodness knows how long. Becker's up on a drugs charge. Markowitz isn't firing on all cylinders. And two others are about to sneak off. What's happening to the partnership?'

'Nonsense, Leland. It may be just a rumour. And if it's true, it may turn out to be a good way of pruning dead wood.'

McKenzie shook his head. 'If people start to think that things are going badly for the firm, they won't put business our way,' he said. 'And with our overheads, we need all the business we can get. We might as well give up. Now, tell me about Becker, just to depress me even more.'

Brackman filled him in on the details, then glanced at his watch and rose to his feet.

'Keep your ear to the ground, Douglas,' McKenzie said. 'I know we don't always see eye to eye, but you're a good guy. And a damned fine lawyer.'

Brackman looked down at the older man, chained to his bed by medical science, and to his surprise felt a flash of pity mingled with sadness. Life wouldn't be the same without Leland. Carefully avoiding the wires, Brackman patted his partner's shoulder before leaving the room.

9

A Royal Audience

Arnie Becker felt like a schoolkid summoned to see the head master. He waited in the luxurious reception area of Gloria Gonzales' office. Telephones buzzed, young men and women bustled around with clipboards and files. A huge poster was pinned up on the wall facing him. It portrayed a chic but painfully thin fashion model whose wide eyes seemed to be staring right at Arnie.

IT'S NOT SMART TO TAKE DRUGS

the poster proclaimed. Another poster showed a group of children surrounding a sleazy-looking man. On this one, the slogan was

ALL DRUG PUSHERS ARE KILLERS

He had been told to arrive for a meeting with Gloria at 5.55 pm. Not 5.45, not 6 o'clock. She certainly had a tight schedule. He had arrived five minutes early, eager not to put a foot wrong. But now he had been waiting for twenty minutes. Maybe this was part of her technique. If it was meant to make him nervous, it certainly worked.

At last, Arnie was led into her office. She sat imperiously in a high-backed chair, not a hair out of place. On television, she always wore low-cut dresses but still managed to appear curiously sexless. Today, she was dressed in a high-necked jacket with gold buttons, almost like a uniform. She tapped the desk with a ruby-red fingernail and fired the first shot.

'I got your letter.'

'Good,' mumbled Arnie, trying on his most winning smile.

'Speak up. You expect me to believe this?' she snapped.

'It's the truth.'

'I can't believe that someone in your position could be so naive.'

Becker vaguely remembered something Victor had said.

'We attorneys sit in our ivory tower and . . .' How the hell did it go? His memory gave up on him. He changed tack. 'You mustn't forget that I don't usually deal with drugs cases. I'm a divorce lawyer. If it had been the colleague who's defending me, Victor Sifuentes, he'd have recognised the signs.'

'So you think Hispanics are a bunch of dopeheads?' Her dark eyes flashed.

'No, no, that's not what I meant at all.' Arnie realised that every time he opened his mouth, he put his foot in it. 'I just meant that, unlike Victor who does a lot of *pro bono* work, I have no experience of the environment of drugs.' A flash of inspiration. 'I'm in exactly the same position as those schookids on the poster outside. I'm a complete innocent in these matters.'

Gloria's face softened. At last he seemed to be getting somewhere.

'So what you said about having drugs planted on you – that wasn't some story you cooked up to sound good in court?' she asked.

'No way. It's the truth, the whole truth and nothing but the truth.' Becker spoke with great feeling, quite different from his usual anodyne tones.

'OK, OK. I believe you. But how do you think it looks from my point of view to have my attorney up on a drugs charge? I spent thousands of dollars on my public image. My P.R. man wanted to fire you as soon as he read your name in *The Clarion*. At least that report didn't mention your profession. Nothing to connect you with me and my divorce.'

'I realise that's a problem, Gloria. It's something my colleagues and I have discussed at length.'

'I bet. Because it won't make McKenzie Brackman look good if I fire you, will it?'

Arnie looked embarrassed. He was feeling all these emotions he had put aside for years. What had happened to his smooth, relaxed image in the last forty-eight hours?

Gloria continued. 'Let's make a deal. It's too bad this case is receiving so much publicity because of that jerk Calvados who likes little girls. But at least that's distracting the newshounds. I'll retain you as my lawyer as long as you make sure you don't get your name in the papers again. Sure, you'll be mentioned in the court report; that's inevitable. But for goodness sake, keep a low profile. If you make the headlines for any reason – or if anything comes up to connect you with me – you're out on your ear.'

Becker was lost for words.

'Now,' Gloria continued. 'How are you going to prove that the drugs were planted on you and that you were wrongfully arrested?'

'I don't know,' Becker replied. 'I haven't any proof. I'll just have to hope the court believes me.'

'Well, as you know, I have some experience in these matters,' said Gloria. 'Let me give you a tip. Ask for a forensic analysis of the drug; it was coke, wasn't it?'

Becker nodded.

'In a plastic bag or loose?'

'In a bag.'

'Well,' Gloria said firmly. 'If it was in a bag, there'll be fingerprints. Anyway, get the drug analysed as well. If the court won't do it, you must insist on an independent lab test. But, like I said, keep a low profile.'

'I'm so grateful to you, Gloria, you have no idea . . .' Arnie said.

'Well, let's hope everything works out OK,' she replied. 'Now I have to go to a meeting about my new project for schoolkids. I'll come and see you in the office tomorrow. Don't forget about my divorce. I want it. I want it fast. And I want it lucrative. Why not set a private investigator on that schmuck who calls himself my husband?' She waved her hand and Becker felt as though he were being dismissed from an audience with the Queen of England.

*

Once she got home, Ann Kelsey took a shower and washed her hair. She didn't feel like getting dressed properly again so she just put on her new tracksuit. Matthew was playing with his building blocks. She knelt down and joined in the game, comforting him when his elaborate skyscraper collapsed. He put his arms round her neck.

'Mommeeee,' he said, fingering the bright red strawberries on her suit.

'Yes, dear.'

He hugged her hard. 'Love you.' A tear trickled

down her cheek and she brushed it away so he wouldn't see.

'I love you too,' she said.

Being with Matthew made her feel so much better; Ann was even laughing when Stuart came home. She greeted him coolly and concentrated on Matthew until he was tucked up in bed.

Ann found Stuart lying on the living room floor practising some relaxation exercises. He was trying every possible means to regain his health after the coronary he had suffered. Ann stood over him. She decided to try a gentle tack first.

'Stuart, who did you have lunch with today?' she enquired sweetly.

He sat up suddenly, the colour flooding into his face.

'Er . . . nobody. Nobody important, that is.'

'Oh, come on, Stuart,' Ann said, feeling her tension increase. 'You're such a terrible liar. I know you had lunch with a woman. Was she a client?'

'Not exactly.'

'Well, was she or wasn't she?'

Stuart looked round the room despairingly, as though hoping that the answer to Ann's question would appear on the walls like the writing at Belshazzar's Feast.

'No . . . yes . . . er . . .'

'How very comprehensive!' Ann snorted. 'Well, if she is a client, no doubt you'll mention her case at the conference tomorrow morning.'

Stuart looked downcast.

'Well, if you haven't anything else to say, I'm going to bed. I suggest you sleep on the couch so you can think about your lunch companion in peace!' Ann stomped out of the room, her eyes again welling with tears.

Alone in the double bed, Ann couldn't sleep. She had dumped Stuart's pyjamas and a pillow on the landing, had heard him creep up the stairs and then down again. He made no attempt to come into the room or even to talk to her through the door.

'Huh!' she thought. 'If he can't even call out an apology . . .'

Despite the fact that Stuart usually stuck his knees and elbows into her when she was trying to get comfortable, Ann found it impossible to settle with all that extra space. Every time she was on the point of drifting off, she thought of Stuart and the way he had looked at That Woman. He never looked at *her* that way now.

Ann remembered the way it used to be. Stuart's astonishment when she had asked him to come home with her during the firm's annual party. She had been feeling so desperate that evening – about her life, her career, everything. Stuart and she had known each other as colleagues for a long time. That first night, they had got to know each other much, much better. It had all been so right. Now, everything seemed wrong.

10

Standing Room Only

Arnie Becker and Victor Sifuentes set off early for court. Arnie wore the smartest of all his well-cut tailor-made suits but had chosen a sober shirt and tie. He didn't want to look too flash. On the way, in the taxi, they discussed Arnie's meeting with Gloria Gonzales.

'She couldn't have been more different yesterday than she was at the first meeting,' Arnie said.

'How do you mean?'

'That first time, she put on this "poor little me" act, as though she had to persuade me to take on her case. Maybe she was rehearsing for her appearance in court. Yesterday, she was terrifying – intimidating. Neither was the way she appears on television.'

'Maybe she has a whole wardrobe of personalities?' Victor said.

'You're right,' he agreed. 'She must have to be pretty tough sometimes to find out some of the information she uses on her show. And other times, maybe she wheedles facts out of people when toughness won't work.'

'That perfect image helps, too,' said Victor. 'I must say, she always looks terrific on television. I caught a glimpse of her when she came into the office and she looked just as good – it's not all artifice.'

'The amazing thing was that, once she'd agreed not to fire me (with strings attached, natch) she started giving me some good advice for the court hearing,' Arnie told him. 'She said you should insist on having the drugs analysed which were supposed to have been found in my pocket, and the plastic envelope finger-printed.'

'Sure, I'll certainly do as she suggests,' said Victor.

'I must say, after the way she spoke on the telephone the other evening, I'm surprised she had anything good to say. I thought she was just going to tell you to go to hell.'

'Me too. What a weird woman she is. Full of surprises,' said Arnie.

'I should have thought of analysing the drugs and checking for fingerprints,' Victor said, 'but my brain's gone numb with all this anxiety over you and Leland.'

'One thing I will say,' Arnie commented. 'I don't envy that husband of Gloria's. Not one little bit.' Then he suddenly smacked his hand against his forehead. '*Oh hell's angels!* She asked me to put a tail on the poor bastard, and I gone clean forgot to organise it.'

'Call Roxanne when we get to the court and she'll do it,' Victor suggested. 'She'd do anything for you, especially at the moment. I had to use a lot of tact to prevent her from coming with us now. Had to say it was vital for her to stay in the office and keep your clients happy while you're in court – which is true, by the way.'

'Yeah, I used the word "indispensable" to keep her at her desk. I can just imagine her getting up and yelling at the judge if she'd come to court. Still, I mustn't knock her – she *is* indispensable.'

Arnie's stomach suddenly churned as he caught sight of the courthouse. 'Ugh, we're there.'

The taxi couldn't get anywhere near the entrance. The crowds were even greater than yesterday; journalists, television crews, mobile studios, fans, groupies and gawpers, all penned in like cattle behind the police lines – most of the men in denim, with Saddam Hussein moustaches; the girls either in skin-tight trousers or mini skirts, tossing their curtains of long henna-coloured Botticelli curls, styled exactly like Andromeda Fulton's hair.

Arnie and Victor had to show their I.D.s to get through the door.

'Wouldn't it be great if they didn't allow me into my own court hearing?' Arnie said joylessly.

When they finally got inside, Arnie had to fight through a crowd of journalists to get to a payphone. He rang Roxanne and asked her to call Sherwoods, the P.I. agency, and get a private investigator on to Gloria Gonzales' current husband. *Twenty-four-hour surveillance, top priority, five-star confidential. For the eyes of himself and the P.I. only. All correspondence by special delivery.* He had to shout to make himself heard above the hubbub.

Then it was time to take their places in the courtroom. Here excitement prevailed, with an ugly undertow of hysteria. Andromeda Fulton fans were massed along one wall, shrieking encouragement to their idol as she appeared through the main entrance, the seething crowds parting in front of her like the Red Sea, their eyes glazed with adoration and longing, as though before a goddess, a Messiah, a glitzy latter-day *Fuehrerin*.

Even the police and the court officials were craning their necks, standing on tiptoe to get a better view. Arnie found the whole scene both degrading and depressing – his W.A.S.P. upbringing coming to the fore.

Meanwhile Victor Sifuentes had pushed his way forward, taking a good look at her face as she passed. 'If that kid's thirteen, my name's Greta Garbo!' he exclaimed.

Arnie was aware of someone waving to him. It was Nina, the psychic chiropodist, who seemed to be treating the hearing as a social occasion – relaxed, laughing, chatting with the people around her.

Adrian Calvados was the first to take the stand – called by his real name, Graham Grubb – a pale shaggy creature, who reminded Arnie of something out of *Planet of the Apes*, not made any more respectable by a tight-fitting dark business suit and a 'quiet' tie.

He faced three charges: possession of narcotics; allowing his premises to be used for the consumption of narcotics; and, last but not least, having sex with a minor – which was joined with the baroque-sounding offence of 'moral turpitude'.

The D.A., a flashy young man known as 'The Shirt' on account of his rich line in Italian linen, made as big a meal as he could out of Calvados, who pleaded guilty to the first two charges, and not guilty to the last two.

While The Shirt chewed him up, with ominous hints of how fragile young minds were being poisoned by the cesspool of moral degradation that was to be found bubbling up through today's so-called 'pop culture', the alleged victim of this bubbling cesspool sat apparently oblivious to everything and everyone.

Andromeda Fulton pouted her bright red lips as though posing for a studio shot, ran her fingers through her curls and constantly re-crossed her amazingly long tanned legs. Victor pointed out the hard-faced woman sitting next to the star.

'I bet that's her mother – the one who pushes her,'

he whispered to Arnie. The woman wore an exotic hat that looked as though it might taste good with lots of cream, and which matched her shocking pink eye make-up.

'Looks like she put her lipstick in the wrong place,' Arnie whispered back.

'Maybe she had her face lifted so many times, those *are* her lips and not her eyes,' Victor joked. Arnie felt grateful to his colleague for at least trying to lower the tension.

Adrian Calvados was committed for trial on the charges relating to Andromeda Fulton; and was granted bail in the sum of a quarter of a million dollars – which had the reporters crashing through the doors, fighting again to get near the telephones. This would be head-lines, coast-to-coast.

Meanwhile, the rest of the proceedings, Arnie noted, came as a merciful anti-climax. As the morning wore on, a tacky procession of minor rock stars, actors, actresses, agents, record producers, models, dudes, hustlers and phonies trooped endlessly up to take the stand, almost all pleading guilty to the 'possession' charge, and each receiving a thousand dollar fine – which for most of them was the equivalent of a nickel's entrance fee for lesser mortals.

Just in front of Arnie was a middle-aged man in a dark woollen suit, silk tie and Gucci shoes. At first Arnie took him for an attorney like himself; then sud-denly recognised the man from the other night who'd been wearing only his socks and shorts.

He watched him take the stand, and The Shirt called out, 'Are you Rocco Danziger?'

93

'Guess so,' the man growled.

'And what is your profession, Mr Danziger?'

A little elf-like man leapt to his feet and said, 'My client, Mr Danziger, is an actor . . .'

The man on the stand hung his head and looked balefully at the judge. 'I'm not an actor, your Honour – and I've got forty-two films to prove it.'

The judge laughed. He was enjoying himself. He fined Rocco Danziger a thousand dollars. Then it was Arnie Becker's turn. How did he plead? '*Not guilty*'.

The judge looked mildly annoyed. Then The Shirt and Victor Sifuentes went up to the bench and stood for some moments in earnest argument, with the judge doing most of the talking. When Victor came away he was frowning. He went up to Arnie on the stand and whispered, 'Seems all the other charges refer to grass. Now the D.A.'s saying you were found with cocaine, which is a much more serious charge. Could even be custodial.'

'Oh God.' Arnie felt his stomach turn over. Victor patted his arm. 'Take it easy.'

It was all over in less than two minutes. Bail was set at five thousand dollars; then Victor, as arranged, asked for an independent analysis of the substance allegedly found in Becker's pocket – something which, surprisingly, no one else had requested – and also that the polythene packet be tested for fingerprints.

Minutes later, the judge banged his gavel and adjourned. Arnie wanted to go to the nearest bar and get smashed; but Victor, still wearing his professional hat as Arnie's attorney, counselled restraint and caution. Douglas Brackman would give them little sympathy if they took any more time off than was absolutely necessary.

As it was, with the crowds still dense in the street, they had to walk nearly four blocks before they found a taxi.

*

'Boy, am I glad to see you!' said Roxanne when they got back to the office. 'The telephone hasn't stopped ringing. Seems every client you ever had has come up with some new problem. Everyone in L.A. is getting divorced. They're all having mid-life crises. At least two divorcees you represented last year have got married in the meantime and want to get divorced again. Oh, and Mr Leyton called and said his ex-wife sawed the dining table in half while he was away in Maine.'

'What the hell was he doing in Maine?' said Arnie crossly. He was feeling exhausted after the morning's tension and the sight of his desk piled with papers made him want to creep away and curl up in a dark corner.

'How should I know? Look, I've made you some chicken sandwiches. That's real good chicken – I roasted it myself last night. None of that store-bought stuff. Hey, how did it go in court?'

'I thought you'd never ask,' said Arnie through a mouthful of chicken. 'Seemed OK. I was totally eclipsed by rock stars and nymphettes. Not to mention psychic chiropodists. At this rate, I'll never make the headlines – thank goodness.' He turned his attention to his in-tray and tried to focus his brain cells.

A few minutes later, Jonathan Rollins and Mike Kuzak came in to ask about the hearing.

'We've just been to see Leland,' Jonathan said. 'He seems kind of low. Hardly surprising, I guess.'

'I think he's still quite confused,' said Mike. 'I don't know what kind of medication he's on. Kept asking us if we were happy.'

'Well, isn't that nice,' cooed Roxanne. 'How wonderful of him to think of others at a time like this.'

'Did he ask about me?' Arnie enquired.

'Well, he spoke about your case, of course,' Jonathan replied. 'Seemed very concerned about proving your innocence and not muddying the name of McKenzie Brackman. He said over and over, "The partnership must stay strong". Almost like an incantation. He was glad to hear Brackman's behind you, anyway.'

'Talking of Brackman, did you see the look he gave us when we came in just now?' Mike asked. 'We hadn't been out that long, though the traffic was bad. He was hanging around near the door like he was on sentry duty.'

'You'd think he has enough to worry about without checking to see how long we're taking for lunch,' said Arnie. 'Now, I must try and get on with some work. I have a meeting with Gloria Gonzales at four and I need to think. That woman doesn't miss a trick.'

*

They drove up into the hills and parked their car in the shade of some pine trees. He took a bottle of champagne from a cooler and unwrapped two fluted glasses which had been protected by a damask napkin. Pressing a button to lower one of the smoked glass windows, he aimed the bottle at the trees and eased out the cork. The pale liquid frothed into their glasses.

She opened an ice-filled silver box in which lay a dozen oysters on the half shell. He picked one up and put it gently into her mouth. She swallowed it and then kissed him hard. They shared the salty taste. When they paused for breath she said, 'Close that window. We don't want anyone to see what we're doing.'

11

Man or Mouse?

Late that afternoon, well after three o'clock, Ann Kelsey found herself in a cab downtown, on her way back from buying some clothes for Matthew, when another cab pulled just in front of hers and she was catapulted forward against the driver's seat, nearly striking her head.

'Sorry, lady! That guy up front should have his licence revoked. If I didn't have you in the cab . . .'

But Ann Kelsey wasn't listening. She was staring out of the window, white in the face, feeling her legs going numb, the tears welling up.

The driver gave a long angry blare on his horn, as he pulled out from behind the stationary taxi, still cursing, '. . . if you weren't in the cab, lady, I'd get out and tell that mother . . . tell the guy . . . !'

But Ann Kelsey was crouching down in the back of the cab, shoulders hunched, her head deep in her hands. She had seen the woman first – a tall, familiar figure with a great cascade of dark red hair, and deeply tanned legs – so long they seemed to start round her shoulders. Ann Kelsey had no time to notice her clothes, except that they had obviously cost a bomb; and her face was enigmatic behind the statutory dark glasses. But Ann remembered thinking afterwards: A woman who looked like that could only be a high-class hooker or the wife of a very rich husband from whom she was playing hookie.

She had one last glimpse of her husband, as he came scuttling up beside the woman and took her arm. Ann Kelsey felt a stab of pain right in her solar plexus, as though she'd been kicked by a mule. The awful thing was, *Stuart looked so ridiculous*. The back of his suit was rumpled, like a relief map of the Himalayas; but perhaps worse, he was at least four inches *shorter* than the woman.

Oh God! she thought, and buried her head in her hands.

'You okay, lady?' The driver, a young Asian, was watching her in his mirror, looking concerned. 'You want me to stop?'

'No. I'd like you to take me home.' She gave him the address, then sat back, trying to compose herself. She felt helpless, wounded. On the run like a hunted animal. She couldn't go back to the office like this – she could feel her make-up running down her face. Anyway, she couldn't face anybody. Least of all, Stuart. Yet could she survive several more hours waiting for him to come home? Perhaps she'd be better checking in to some hotel? But that was only postponing the final, inevitable showdown.

Little Matthew was still with the baby-minder. Ann Kelsey usually rang when she was free for him to be brought home. Today, she'd ring late. Although it was still only just after four, she didn't want her baby to see her like this – for she was convinced that even infants picked up vibes of emotion, sometimes even more acutely than some adults.

Back at their house which, she remembered with a sickening thump, was in their joint names – Stuart having insisted on this, in the first flush of married bliss – she tried to distract herself by doing some frantic cleaning and dusting and scouring; then, exhausted, she went up and had a long hot bath.

She was determined that Stuart should not find her

102

like this. She spent some care reapplying her make-up and bathing her eyes. But they still looked puffy and slightly red. Then she started worrying about how, in real life, people went about these things – how they broached the subject, and which tack she should then take? Poor Arnie would know. Should she call him? Although he had his hands full at the moment, God help him!

If he wasn't almost on his deathbed, she might have consulted Leland McKenzie. There was a solid pillar of virtue and common sense on which she could lean for comfort and advice; but even that avenue was closed.

Oh God! she thought, I feel so *miserable*. She climbed out of the bath and stood for some time examining herself in the mirror. She still had a fine body. She bet she had just as good a body as that expensively wrapped bitch she'd seen getting out of the taxi. Then she started getting angry. What had *that woman* got that she hadn't? And little Stuart, of all people! What on earth did a girl like that *see* in him? He wasn't all that hot in bed, for Chrissake! Maybe she had some kind of fetish about very small, middle-aged men? They say it takes all sorts . . . But *this*? Even in California . . .

She started dressing; and as she did so, she realised she was dressing to kill. A pair of black bikini briefs with lace edging, high-heels, and a loose linen shirt which revealed the tops of her naked breasts. It was still only a quarter to six. And she realised, with another rush of anger, that even if he wasn't out screwing a 'client', he still didn't usually make it home until around seven-thirty, or even later, if the traffic was bad.

103

She decided to go downstairs and watch a movie. But first she called the baby-minder and asked if she could keep Matthew until after eight. She felt a bit of a heel doing it, but this was a priority. In any case, the baby-minder said Matthew had been out to Griffith Park and was now fast asleep. Ann Kelsey didn't feel so bad. She could concentrate her energies on Stuart.

On reflection, she decided that her *apres-bain* outfit might be rather overdoing it – she was certainly not in the mood to seduce her husband – and had started upstairs, when she heard the click and grinding of the locks in the front door. She stood halfway up the stairs, transfixed.

Supposing he was bringing *her* home? Of course, it was out of the question. He'd know she'd be at home. Unless, of course, he wanted to have the final showdown, here, now . . . She found that her whole body was quivering with nerves. She couldn't move, up or down, terrified that her legs would collapse under her.

Stuart came in. He didn't see her at first. He was alone and walked over to the hall table to see if there was any mail for him. He picked up a couple of envelopes, then turned towards the stairs, as he always did, intending to have a shower.

He stopped, stared at her, then chuckled – more in surprise than pleasure. Somehow she found this both patronising and too carefree by half.

'Jesus, honey, what have I done to deserve this? You look terrific!' She thought of saying right out what he deserved. Instead, she wrapped the shirt closely round her and took a tentative step down. Anger had defused the worst of her nerves. 'Have a good day, did you?' she said.

'Oh usual, honey. With both Leland and Arnie out of commission, things get pretty hectic. I was going to bring some work home, but I'm bushed. And you know what Dr Gormley said . . . ?'

'No. What did Dr Gormley say?' she asked, through clenched teeth.

Stuart seemed a little put out by this. 'Hell, honey, I really do watch it. The cholesterol, I mean. And I'm *not* taking on too much at the office. You know that.'

She had reached the foot of the stairs now. 'I'm not talking about the office, Stuart. You must take me for a goddam fool! Perhaps I *am* a goddam fool!'

Stuart Markowitz looked perplexed. 'Honey, I don't know . . .'

'Oh stop pretending, Stuart! I can stand the truth. What I can't stand is your wimpish lying!'

'Lying? When have I lied?'

'Your lunch date, Stuart. Twice, at the very least. Have you forgotten her name already? C'mon, Stuart, what is it?'

Stuart Markowitz had gone an unhealthy grey colour, like wet cement. 'You mean –' He took two leaden steps and sank down into the nearest chair. 'Mrs Emily Stallwood . . .' he croaked.

'That's the one! You were both unlucky, Stuart. I was in the cab right behind yours, when you were dropped near the City Hall this afternoon.'

'I was dropping her off. Emily's a client.'

'Emily Smallwood is a whore!' she yelled, coming

105

closer, hands on her half-naked hips. 'Just look me in the eye! Are you a man – or a mouse?'

'I'm a mouse, I guess,' Stuart said miserably. 'I mean, if I wasn't a mouse, I wouldn't be married to you.'

'And what the *hell* does that mean?'

Stuart trembled; he'd never seen her like this before. Come to think of it, he couldn't remember having ever seen her angry with him before. He felt giddy and slightly sick.

'Well?' She came marching up to him, pausing a couple of feet away. 'Who, Stuart – *who* is Emily Smallwood? I want to know right now. Because if I have to find out later, it'll be all the worse for you!'

'God, honey, I dunno – I just can't believe all this . . .'

'Nor could I believe it this afternoon, when I saw you getting out of that cab. So that makes two of us!!'

'Oh my God.' Stuart lowered his head into his hands. 'Oh God!' He began to sob. 'She's a client. Please, you must believe me. She's just a client.'

'Oh yeah? Well I don't believe you.'

'Please, Ann, you must!' He raised his hands and his eyes were wet with tears. At that moment, he reminded her of a small dog who's been caught out by its owner in some atrocious transgression. He was cowering, waiting for the next outburst. He didn't have to wait long.

'Since when do you meet clients for lunch and drop them off in taxis?'

'You don't understand . . .' he began.

'Damn right I don't! I wouldn't mind so much if you had the guts to come clean. Anyway, it's not the first time, is it? I've seen her with you before.'

106

Stuart sank his head back in his hands. 'I – I – I just can't believe it . . .'

'Believe what?'

'I just can't believe you don't trust me. *Me!* Your husband!'

'Why should I trust you when you take strange women out to lunch – and can't give me an explanation. You – Stuart Markowitz, a top L.A. lawyer – and you can't even explain something as simple as this. You're pathetic!'

'I *have* explained it! I've told you – she's a client!'

'Oh yeah. And what sort of case is it? C'mon, Stuart, since when did you do divorce work for McKenzie Brackman?'

'It's got nothing to do with divorce.'

'Oh no?' She stood over him, strong and half-naked, and he seemed to flinch under her gaze. 'Well, what does Mrs Stallwood want from you that she can't get from anyone else?'

'Emily – I mean, Mrs Smallwood – needs advice of a highly complicated nature about her tax position.'

She nodded. 'Right. Now I'm going to tell you what I'm going to do. I'm going upstairs to finish dressing, and in the meantime I expect you to pack whatever you need and leave this house. I am not sleeping under the same roof as you one more night!' And with that she stomped off up the stairs.

When she got to the bedroom, she found she was trembling so much that she could hardly stand. And another thing worried her – Stuart's colour. He had every reason to look pale, but now he'd been looking positively ill. And she remembered what nice Dr Gormley had said – about taking too much exercise – undue exertion. And she guessed that servicing Mrs Stallwood would hardly rate a gentle stroll in the country. *Emily Stallwood* – what a ridiculous name! It sounded like the heroine of some 19th-century English novel.

She took her time dressing. Once or twice she thought she heard her husband moving about, collecting his things from the bathroom, packing some papers – it was like the other night, only even more furtive. Perhaps it would have been better if he could have got mad and they'd had a blazing row – something . . . something positive, if nothing more. But Stuart was so – so – so *mousy*, as he'd admitted himself. Was she so domineering? she wondered. Had she made him feel so inadequate that he had to run off after call-girls? And how much did a woman like that *cost*?

When she'd finished in front of the mirror, she realised that her mascara had run again and she looked flushed and angry, like one of those harridans who were always trying to get their alimony jacked up. And she started to cry again.

A moment later she heard a faint tap at the door. 'Ann?'

'Yes – what do you want?'

'I'm going out now – as you suggested. I'll probably stay at the Athletic Club. And if they don't have room, I'll go to a hotel.'

'What's wrong with *chez* Stallwood? Or I suppose she's married, and the husband might rough you up?'

There was a pause. 'Good-bye, Ann.'

She didn't answer; instead, waited for his barely audible footsteps to pad downstairs – then the heavy noise of the outside door closing. She guessed he'd take his own car – a rather small, old European model which she's always felt exactly suited him.

She sat down on the bed and began to weep – no longer sobs of rage or frustration, but this time of deep, terrible grief. She'd never known before that she loved Stuart so much.

12

On Stony Ground

Stuart Markowitz got to the office next morning nearly half an hour before his wife. Douglas Brackman was loping about near the door to the lifts, like some ageing wolf who scents that all is not well.

Stuart looked awful – worse than he'd ever looked since leaving hospital. Grey-faced, crumpled, abject. Brackman wondered if he ought to send him home. The man certainly didn't look up to facing a client.

But if Brackman thought Stuart didn't look too hot this morning, he wasn't prepared for how his wife looked. Ann Kelsey wore a bright Hermes scarf to conceal her lank, dishevelled hair, and very black sunglasses to hide her eyes, which were puffed and reddened from crying and lack of sleep. She came into the office almost at a run, muttered something to Brackman which he didn't catch, then disappeared into the Ladies.

Douglas Brackman didn't need a university degree in psychology to know that all was not well between Mr and Mrs Markowitz. It was at moments like this, he felt, when he longed for those dear dead halcyon days when women stayed at home and idled away the day singing and hanging up the washing. Or whatever.

It was a couple of minutes before ten o'clock. Conference time. He went through and took the chair at the head of the table, which was usually reserved for Leland McKenzie. A moment later Arnie Becker and Victor Sifuentes came in together, followed by Abby Perkins, then Michael Kuzak, and a full minute later, Stuart Markowitz.

Brackman's baleful eye surveyed them along each

113

side of the table. 'Stuart – where's Ann? Not sick, I hope?'

'No,' he said, in a tiny croak. 'No, she's fine.'

Brackman glared, fidgetting with his silver pencil. 'Well – we'd better start. Arnie – everything okay?'

'Okay,' said Arnie, nodding wearily.

'We sent the plastic bag and the powder off for an independent analysis,' Sifuentes said.

Brackman looked hard at Arnie Becker. 'And how's that dreadful woman, Gloria Gonzales?'

'Well, she's being surprisingly tolerant and helpful, under the circumstances.'

'Let's keep it that way,' Brackman said, and looked up as Ann Kelsey came in. He watched her choose the chair that was furthest from her husband, where she could not easily meet his eye.

'Look, Ann,' Brackman's voice was smooth and commanding. 'This ship is at least one crew member short. And as Victor here is having to keep another crew member from going under, we are – if you'll pardon the naval metaphors – a ship that's more than just a little short-handed. One more defection and we'll be the *Marie Celeste*.' He paused, watching Ann Kelsey like a cobra watching a rabbit, then turned to her husband. 'Stuart' – this time it was the cobra watching a squirrel – 'if you and Ann have hit a stony patch . . .'

Stuart Markowitz gave a sad smile. 'Between a rock and a hard place, you mean?'

'Well?' Brackman looked from him back to his wife. 'Ann –'

Ann Kelsey suddenly stood up, almost upsetting her chair, and ran from the room. There was an agonised silence. Stuart Markowitz looked as though he were about to crawl under the table.

'Maybe we'd better talk after the conference, Stuart. It doesn't look as though you or your wife are up to making much of a contribution, anyway.'

Stuart stood up, mumbled something, and crept out.

Brackman looked back down the table. 'Well, Abby. How's the glamorous Russian Prince?'

'He's a Count. Or says he is. And he's driving me up the wall.'

'He's obsessed by her,' Kuzak said. 'He wants to marry her and take her off to his palace in St Petersburg. And there'll be dancing till dawn . . .'

'Okay,' said Brackman. 'Joke's over. Any of you bright guys know what gives with Mr and Mrs Markowitz?'

'You want to know something round here,' said Kuzak. 'Better ask Roxanne.'

'I will,' Brackman said grimly. 'Now let's try and get some work done . . .'

*

Late that evening Douglas Brackman called at the hospital to see Leland McKenzie, and found Abby Perkins already there. He smiled grimly. 'Hello everybody! – is McKenzie Brackman moving into new offices here at the Alhambra Hospital?'

The joke got the reception it deserved. Abby tittered politely, while Leland McKenzie looked sourly over the top of his new bifocals which were clinging precariously to the end of his nose. 'So – more grapes?' he growled.

He already had five bunches littered about the room in small bowls. Brackman had bought him a new book about Venice. It weighed at least a couple of kilos.

McKenzie lifted it. 'Hey, Douglas, you could kill someone with this! Anyway, thanks. I'll enjoy reading it, when I get round to fixing up a hoist. So, what gives?'

Brackman looked warily at Abby, as if to say, Not in front of the children.

'It's all right,' said McKenzie. 'Abby's told me the whole story. Or at least as much as she thought my health would stand.'

'Ah!' Brackman looked discomforted. If there was nothing he liked more, it was knowing a secret. It was even better than gossip. And in this case, it was a combination of both. He looked accusingly at Abby, who blushed.

'Tell him, Abby,' McKenzie said. 'The old firm's falling apart. Tell him.'

Abby said, 'I didn't come here to tell stories. I mean, I really came to ask Leland's advice on how to handle this crazy Russian I've got . . .'

'Yes all right, Abby,' said Brackman. 'Cut the commercials.'

'Well,' – she looked to McKenzie for moral support – 'Ann Kelsey told me all about it, and she was so upset she had to go home, so I thought I ought to get some advice.'

Brackman looked at McKenzie. He was sitting up in bed, surrounded by a panoply of files, papers, dictating machines, portable computer-cum-word-processor, and several law books and magazines. Brackman said,

'So what glad tidings did little Miss Perkins bring you, Leland?'

Abby sucked in her breath in a sharp hiss, and her neat little features flushed darkly, as she stood up. 'I must be getting along,' she said quickly. 'I've got a meeting with my Count tomorrow.' She gave Leland a quick peck on the cheek, then hurried out of the room, with scarcely a glance at Brackman.

'You've upset her,' McKenzie said. 'You really must try to understand that women – even pretty young women – are still members of the human race.'

'I just didn't think it would get out so quickly.'

'Okay. How bad is it?'

'Well, it's bad, that's for sure. Ann Kelsey's convinced he's having a relationship with this new client of his, Emily Stallwood.'

'Yeah, that much I know. But surely? – I mean, *not Stuart*? Unless we've all totally misjudged him.'

'Well that's how I looked at it,' Brackman said. 'But not Ann Kelsey. Apparently she's convinced he's being unfaithful.'

'But how? I mean, how did she get on to it?'

'As luck would have it,' Brackman said, 'she saw them both downtown – not once, but *twice*, for Chrissake!'

'*Is* she a client?'

'Yes – as far as I know.'

'You mean, you *don't know*?' cried McKenzie, looking genuinely shocked. 'You're the senior partner – you're captain of the ship. It's your job to know *everything* that happens!'

Brackman held up his hand. 'It's not like that,

117

Leland. Stuart's client is married to a very rich man who has his money scattered in a number of places and she wants some confidential advice on tax – which, as we all know, is where Stuart shines brightest.'

'Okay, so what's his problem then?'

Brackman frowned. 'I'm sworm to secrecy, Leland.'

'Oh yea – you and half the office, I guess?'

'Abby doesn't know, does she?'

It was Leland McKenzie's turn to frown; he not only looked worried, but angry too. 'All she told me was that Ann Kelsey seems to be close to a breakdown, and her husband has moved out of the house. And the reason – the oldest one in the world. *Another woman*.' He gave Brackman a hard stare. 'That the reason she gave you?'

'Well, as a matter of fact, Leland' – he shifted his weight on the bed, aware that his right buttock had gone numb – 'I didn't talk to her. I talked to Stuart. What he told was in the utmost confidence. And even then, he only gave me the bones of the story.'

'Okay, let's have the bones then,' Leland McKenzie said wearily.

Brackman began. 'Mrs Emily Stallwood is married to a one-time movie mogul, Marcus Stallwood, who is seriously rich. He has homes here in California, the Caymans, Switzerland, London and Morocco.'

'Sure you haven't missed one?' Leland McKenzie said, with his sour grin.

'Probably. From his wife's point of view – legally – he's domiciled in Switzerland. But he has been born and brought up in London, and only came Stateside in the early sixties. Now the nub of it is this. Mrs Stallwood – who is, by all accounts, a very lovely woman, at least to look at – wants out. I don't know the details, and nor does Stuart. But her main concern is that if she divorces him, she wants a fair slice of the action. Trouble is, Boy Marcus has bank accounts all over the world, and as sure as I'm sitting on this bed, the moment he knows she's filed for divorce – or even suspects it – whatever money he has here in the States will be as dust in the wind.'

'And is our Stuart up to unravelling this charming mystery?'

'That only time can tell. But Mrs Emily Stallwood obviously hopes he can.'

'What I still don't understand,' said Leland, is why Ann Kelsey has to go to pieces over this? I mean, can't he just explain that she's a client and that the work is highly confidential?'

'Well I'd have thought so too. But according to Stuart, he has told her – several times – and she *doesn't believe him*!'

'It's ridiculous,' snapped Leland. 'She's a sensible girl, Ann – unless, of course . . .'

'No,' said Brackman. 'Not Stuart, surely . . .'

'Women do have strange and wonderful ways,' mused Leland. 'After all, Ann Kelsey fell for him. So maybe this sex-bomb who's fed up with her husband has decided that Stuart can fulfil two roles for the price of one?'

'It's possible, I suppose,' Brackman murmured, without conviction. 'I tend to believe Stuart. He's too guileless, too innocent – and, I have to say, he doesn't have the balls. As far as Ann Kelsey's concerned, Stuart has had the appalling bad luck of being seen by his wife, not once but *twice* in the space of a few days, obviously both times having lunch downtown with a sex-bomb.'

'So why didn't Mrs Stallwood come to the office and consult Stuart there?'

'Because,' said Brackman, 'according to Stuart, she's terrified her husband will find out she's been seeing lawyers.'

'But she's been seeing a lawyer in taxis and restaurants?' said Leland.

'Sure, sure,' said Brackman gloomily. 'But I suppose it's different in a restaurant – different, I mean, to walking into the elevator and riding up to the eighth floor and going into the offices of McKenzie Brackman.'

'Well, Ann Kelsey thinks so, anyway. Know what I'm going to do, Douglas? I'm going to call the senior nurse and give her a forty-eight hour ultimatum. I'll tell her that things aren't much quieter *here* than at the office. Forty-eight hours, then I'm discharging myself!'

'Sorry, Leland. This hasn't exactly been a rest hour.'

'Wouldn't want it any other way, Douglas. I'd die of boredom.'

*

Brackman got back to the office, hot and sticky from the early rush hour, knowing he had at least three hours' work ahead of him, if he was to have any chance of clearing the backlog. And that was not including any phone calls from outside.

He asked Jayne – one of the dizzy 'Valley Girls' at the reception desk – to bring him a pot of fresh black coffee. Then he removed his jacket, turned up the air-conditioning, and started into a new pile of documents on his desk.

Then the phone rang. 'Brackman,' he growled.

'Hello, Mr Brackman! I am Lotte Schnitzel, and I am very happy to speak with you . . .'

'Who?'

'Lotte Schnitzel. You gave me your card. You were so very kind.'

It took Brackman a few more seconds before the penny dropped. The old lady out of gas. He adjusted his scowl, and said, in his nicest voice, 'It was my pleasure. I hope you got home all right?'

'Yes, well as a matter of fact I had a very interesting experience because after you'd . . .' She was off; and Brackman held the phone away from his ear, while her voice droned on, less like clotted cream this time, and more like an angry wasp trapped in the mouthpiece.

He offered up a little plaintive prayer, as Jayne trotted in with the coffee. 'Thanks, honey!' – then into the phone: 'It's all right, Mrs Schnitzel – yes, yes, *Fraulein* Schnitzel – I was talking to someone in the office . . . Yes. Yes, yes . . .'

As Jayne left, he noticed that her skirt was provocatively short, her little behind enticingly round. He waited for her to close the door, then gathered up enough courage to cut into the endless flow from the phone. 'Fraulein Schnitzel, I happen to be very busy at the moment . . .'

'That is what I am phoning about. You see, I know from my work that you lawyers have many, many tremendous pressures in your work – you have terrific

121

responsibilities, and your social relationships with your clients . . .'

'Fraulein Schnitzel, I don't quite see . . .'

'Actually, as a point of fact, I am only Fraulein Schnitzel to my clients. My married name is Kurtz, but of course . . .'

'Mrs Kurtz, what exactly has this to do with me?'

'Well this I explain. But first, I prefer that you call me Fraulein Schnitzel. It is more professional.'

Brackman found himself holding the phone as though it were a weapon. And if Mrs Kurtz, *nee* Schnitzel, had been in the room, he might well have used it.

'Fraulein Schnitzel,' he said, as though speaking to a small child. 'What exactly *is* your profession?'

'I am a psycho-therapist,' she replied, in triumph, as though this heralded a cure for all his ills. 'So you see, I can help you and your colleagues in all possible ways. For a start . . .'

Brackman held away the phone again, then noticed that Jayne had brought him a sachet of artificial sweeteners instead of sugar. He pressed his intercom: 'Roxanne! This your doing, isn't it? Tell Jayne I like my coffee *with two spoonfuls per cup. Capisce?*'

Fraulein Schnitzel's voice was still going strong, like an uncapped oil well in Kuwait. '. . . I can arrange for separate sessions for the female staff to discuss their problems caused by the male staff, although it is my experience that after a short time, both sexes will welcome integrated . . .'

'Fraulein Schnitzel, it's very, very kind of you. But you see, I'd have to discuss the matter with my partners . . .'

122

'Of course, yes, I understand, but first why . . .'

'Why don't you put it all in writing and send it me? Yes. Yes, me too. Thank you, Fraulein Schnitzel!'

He sank back and stared at the little blonde in front of him – was it Jayne or Candice? He was never quite sure. The girl giggled. 'You made Roxanne real mad just now.' She was holding a packet of sugar in her hands. 'She says this stuff'll kill you!'

'That, my dear girl, is precisely why I want it!'

13

A Couch Potato
Grows Roots

When Arnie Becker got back to his small, snug apartment in Santa Monica he was bushed. The days of worry since the 'bust' on the beach party had taken their toll. Besides the initial humiliation after the arrest, there was now the ordeal of having to co-exist with his colleagues in the firm. Not only that; apart from a traffic misdemeanour many, many years ago, Arnie had never had cause to consult a lawyer – until now. And he hated it.

Although he rubbed along well enough with Victor Sifuentes – in fact, in normal times they were pretty good buddies – he now found him something like a pain in the ass. What's more, when he told Victor this, he had just laughed and said, 'That's the way it goes, Arnie! It's like medicine – if it tastes nice, it ain't doing you any good!'

But the worst part, he found, was that however hard they denied it, he knew that his colleagues – even Sifuentes – did not entirely believe him. On top of that, he was having to wait at least another forty-eight hours for the independent lab test on the suspect packet that was found in his pocket.

All in all, Arnie felt depressed and listless. It was not a mood he was used to, nor did he intend to endure it a moment longer than necessary. He washed up some old coffee cups in the tiny kitchenette off the main room, mixed himself a Bloody Mary, with plenty of tabasco sauce, then put on an ancient LP of a Buck Clayton jam-session. That usually did the trick; but this evening he seemed out of luck. One minute into the record the phone rang. He decided not to answer, but knew that it took an iron will to leave a ringing phone;

besides, as the mighty jazzmen got into their stride, the ringing tones were almost obliterated . . . Ten, eleven, twelve . . . But Hell! he couldn't stand it anymore . . . For someone to be this persistent, it must be something important. Important for the other party, of course, not for him.

He grabbed the portable telephone and grunted into the mouthpiece, 'Becker.'

'Hi Arnie! Howwya!'

'Who?' He could barely hear above the music.

'It's Sally. You haven't forgotten?'

'How could I *ever* forget?' He carried the phone across to the hi-fi deck and turned down the volume. 'So. Sally. What is it?'

'Just to say I been feeling so awful about the other night.'

'I haven't been feeling too good about it myself,' Arnie said.

'I guess you must've thought I set you up?'

'Frankly, I haven't thought about you at all.'

She giggled, and said in her tweety-pie voice, 'I guess I deserved that! But honest, how can I make it up to you?'

'By not asking me to any more parties.'

There was a silence down the line. Then she said softly, 'Arnie, I like you a lot. D'ya know that?'

'I don't know and I don't care.'

'Oh Arnie, don't be like that. Please. You were such a perfect gentleman the other night.'

'You mean, I didn't make love to you in the surf?'

She giggled again, nervously this time. 'Are you sure I can't make it up to you?'

128

'Yes. But you can go some of the way by telling me why you invited me in the first place. Or was I the *only* available male in your book that night?'

Another pause. Becker had an image of her the other end, sucking her thumb as she tried to think up the next coy remark. 'I'm so lonesome, Arnie. And it's such beautiful night – the stars are all out. I could cook you something, and then . . .' She hesitated. 'We could smoke some pot, Arnie. I got some really good stuff – Jamaican gold.'

'Listen, Sally. Get this into your skull. I'm a lawyer – and a successful one, for the moment. And I do not – repeat *not* smoke pot. *Compris?*'

He imagined her chewing her finger now, her interest in him exacerbated by his stonewall resistance. There was no doubt that Sally was sexy. Very sexy. But she was also, he suspected, slightly crazy. And here another image presented itself: Sally as the rejected mistress in the film *Fatal Attraction*; for, like half the young males in the United States, Arnie had watched the film with a kind of horrified awe.

A nutcase who took drugs and had sex on the brain – that was all Arnie Becker needed as he wearily approached the mid-life crisis. But having decided she was crazy, he was careful not to upset her anymore than absolutely necessary.

'By the way, how come you didn't get busted the other night?' he asked her.

'I was smart. I hid under the bed in the spare room.'

'Very smart. Wish I'd thought of it myself.' He was preparing to terminate the conversation, when she said, 'Arnie, I haven't been totally honest with you.'

He groaned inwardly. 'I find people rarely are,' he said.

She giggled again. 'I like you, Arnie! You're so funny.'

Hilarious, he thought. *What am I doing talking to this cookie?* He waited.

After what seemed several minutes, but was most likely about thirty seconds, she said, 'I wasn't honest with you the other night either. You see, I'd bust up with my boyfriend. He works as a stuntman for the studios. Freelance, he won't be tied to any one company. He's a loner, see – and gorgeous. The hunky type, and real mean when he feels like it.'

Arnie Becker said nothing.

'Well you see,' she went on. 'He's a friend of Adrian Calvados. They're both into the drug scene real big.'

At that moment Arnie wondered if it was paranoia, but could it be his phone was bugged? That someone really had set him up? He said warily, 'Should you be telling me all this, Sally?'

'Well I wanted to explain. You see my guy – he's called Rock Stone . . . Don't you think that's good – *Rock Stone*?'

'I think it's wonderful, Sally. But what's Mr Stone got to do with the party?'

'Well, I was going on his invite. Then we had a row and he said he wouldn't take me. So I rang you and you took me. Neat, eh?'

'Very neat. I should think of setting up an escort agency.'

'Oh yes, you'd be wonderful! I'd tell all my friends.'

'Was this Rock Stone at the party?' Arnie asked.

130

'No. Like I said, he was being mean that night. He's still being mean.'

'What you're saying, Sally, is you're using me to try and make him jealous.'

There was a pause. 'I just didn't think about it like that,' she said at last. 'I really wanted you that night. I bet I could have got you if the cops hadn't spoiled things. I've wanted you ever since that first time we met, at the Getty Museum event.' Another pause. 'You could come over here. I'm not far from you.'

'Sounds lovely, Sally, but unfortunately . . .'

'I've got on some lovely satin briefs. Want to know what colour they are?'

'. . . I've got a very boring date, I'm afraid – it's to do with work.'

She giggled. 'A date to do with work? You're cute, Arnie! And you know something . . . my briefs are purple. Purple satin!'

'Sally, I have to go now.'

'I could wait till your date's over and come out to you then?'

'No, Sally. No – no. I'm sorry . . .'

'Oh, you're like all the others – you like to fit in your love-life when it's convenient! Yeah, well you can go boil your head!' And to Arnie's overwhelming relief, the line went dead.

Arnie went over to the kitchenette and drank a long glass of iced water. He found he was sweating slightly.

14

Sugar And Spice

They met by chance at one of those Hollywood parties at which the world and his wife want to be seen; quite a lot of the world arrived with other people's wives . . . However, on this occasion they were each with their respective spouses. The hostess, Francesca Fox, whose deep tan and light hair colour had both come out of bottles, introduced them.

'Yes, I believe we have met a few times,' the woman said, graciously extending a hand whose nails had been newly sculpted that morning. He pressed her hand with his and spoke with his eyes as well as his lips.

They murmured small talk at each other for several minutes, uttering the inanities used by strangers. Flash bulbs popped and brilliant white, capped teeth gleamed in fixed, humourless smiles. Gradually, the others in their group moved away though they remained within earshot of many guests, since the room was tightly packed with 'rich white trash'.

He took a flute of champagne from a passing waiter's tray and handed it to her with a gallant bow.

'How many husbands has Francesca had now?' she asked. 'I've lost count.'

'Either four or five,' he said. 'The one before last was a toy-boy but I can't remember whether she actually married him. Number three was a real catch, of course. He died only six months after their wedding and left her the lot.'

'She should be so lucky!'

'Have you seen the wonderful art collection she inherited?' he asked.

'Why, no,' she said. 'Though I've heard she has a lot of Old Masters. I'd be interested to see them.'

'I'd be delighted to show you,' he replied. 'There are many Impressionists too. I believe there is even a Pisarro in one of the bathrooms.'

'Then why don't we look at that first?' She slid an elegant brown arm through his and they pushed through the crowd, the women in their tight designer dresses proving that one *can* be too rich and too thin.

They found the picture hanging, as he had said, in the small but sumptuously-decorated room, its walls hung with rich dark velvet, the accoutrements in marble decorated with gilt lions heads. The oil painting glowed as though illuminated.

'Well, isn't that just wonderful,' she said. 'But you know, I find the noise of the party distracting. I think I could appreciate it more with the door closed . . .

*

The next hearing of Arnie Becker's case was set for Friday, some time in the afternoon. Brackman said it was a good time, since it minimised the chance of saturation coverage by the media: it was the beginning of the weekend, so most journalists were either out of town or concentrating on the sports fixtures.

Then, in the morning, Sifuentes burst in. 'Arnie, the lab's come through. And you know what? The stuff was icing sugar!'

'*What?*'

'I know. Real weird. What's more, there were only two sets of prints on the bag, and neither of them are yours.'

'Phew! I could do with a drink, Victor.'

136

They didn't discuss the matter further until they were in their nearest watering hole, a very large, crowded, noisy room with batteries of blinding spotlights and minimalist furniture, like a film studio. The walls were covered in muzzy monochrome photographs and there was a sign above the bar: *THE CLIENTELE IS REQUESTED NOT TO USE PORTABLE TELE-PHONES ON THE PREMISES*. This request was being assiduously ignored. Sifuentes grabbed a waitress with wet corkscrew curls and dark red eyeshadow and asked for two schooners of Czechoslovakian beer. They had to shout to make themselves heard.

'So what the hell is going on, Victor?'

'Deep waters, Watson!' Sifuentes yelled.

'*What?*'

'A literary reference, Arnie my friend!' The beers arrived and they had to drink with their elbows tucked tightly to their sides, rolling on the balls of their feet to avoid being toppled in the crush. 'If I had to make a bet, I'd say you were set up, Arnie.'

'But why icing sugar?'

'Maybe they just wanted to annoy you.'

'But who'd want to annoy me?' Arnie took a long cook drink and thought about Sally. Sally was cookie enough to do most things, but even she couldn't have known the party was going to be raided – *unless, of course, she'd been working as a stoolie*.

Then he remembered something else. The Vice Squad officer at the party – Lieutenant Saxby. He slapped his forehead. 'Jeez, why didn't I think of it before? Guy in charge of the raid – name of Saxby – had a wife I subpoenaed a few years back in a divorce case. She turned out to be a call-girl working out of a hotel in Malibu – earning ten times his salary, with a mink coat, a white convertible – you name it. The poor sap even got investigated for corruption, on account of her lifestyle.'

'In the divorce business,' Sifuentes said, 'you're bound to make enemies.'

'Yeah, but – *if it was Saxby* – how'd he have known I was going to that party? I mean, I didn't know until after it had begun. That girl, Sally – could she have been part of it?'

'I dunno. It'd be difficult to prove, if I got her on the stand.'

'No, for Chrissake don't do that! She'd do for my professional reputation what the Boston Strangler did for door-to-door salesmen!'

'My guess, for what it's worth,' Sifuentes said, '– and guessing's a dangerous habit in the law business – is that when this Lieutenant Saxby recognised you, he decided to pay you back in kind, and make life as unpleasant for you as you had for him. So he planted the packet and let you sweat it out.'

'Well he's sure succeeded there,' said Arnie. 'But why icing sugar?'

'Well' – Sifuentes gave an elegant gesture with his hands – 'planting dope on a suspect is a high-risk game, even for the L.A.P.D.'

'So what's your strategy?'

'I'll try and have a little word with Lieutenant Saxby when we get to court. He won't want the sordid details of his marriage made public again, any more than you'd like it suggested you were a "user". But I'd give you

138

evens one set of those prints on the packet is the Lieutenant's.'

*

It worked like a dream, just as Victor Sifuentes had
promised. They got to the courthouse with half an hour
to spare. Outside, there was the usual screaming rabble
of fans and sensation-seekers pressed against the
crush-barriers, on the off chance they might catch a
further glimpse of Adrian Calvados and Andromeda
Fulton, plus their awful entourage.

But the hearing today was to deal with the nonentities in the haul – mostly those who'd already agreed to
cop a plea of guilty. Sifuentes got them both in through
the side entrance, where they mingled with the scrum
of attorneys and their clients. The atmosphere was fetid
and tacky, with that unmistakeable atmosphere of tension, menace and no-hope that pervades every police
station, every courthouse in the world.

Arnie Becker, used to the more genteel horrors of
the divorce courts, found it deeply depressing. He felt
grubby, unclean – almost an outcast. If anyone had
wanted to make him really miserable, they could have
chosen no better way than with that small packet of
icing.

Sifuentes told him to wait just outside the door – no
point in exhibiting him in front of his peers, some of
whom would no doubt recognise him. Arnie was
impressed by Sifuentes' smooth efficiency, now that he
was seeing the law from the other side of the glass.

After a couple of minutes a voice crackled over the

tannoy system: '*Will Lieutenant Saxby of the Santa Monica Precinct please make contact with the D.A.'s Desk.*' The message was being repeated as Sifuentes rejoined him outside. 'I've arranged for you to be called first. The D.A.'s got the exhibit and they know we're contesting. So now I'm going to talk to Saxby. Take a stroll, get yourself a cup of coffee, get back here in fifteen minutes.'

'Thanks, Victor.'

'It's all on the firm.'

*

Arnie was relieved to see that the court was only about half full. There were a few freaks and juvenile ravers in the public gallery, but on the press benches, he noticed, there seemed to be only two reporters, one with his head down, the other yawning.

'Call Mr Arnold Becker!'

The judge gave Arnie scarcely a glance. 'This the possession of narcotics case, number four-one-eight, Mr Lattimer?'

A smooth young man bounced to his feet and said unctuously, 'It is most certainly, your Honour.'

The judge looked over his rimless bifocals. 'This a change of plea, is it?'

Sifuentes rose. 'That is correct, your Honour. My client will be pleading Not Guilty.'

The judge nodded and made a note. 'Carry on, Mr Lattimer.'

Here Sifuentes rose again. 'Your Honour, I understand that due to the nature of some forensic evidence that has just come into our possession, I shall be submitting, on behalf of my client, that there is no case to answer.'

The judge looked irritated. He wanted to be off in time to get in a few strokes at the Rancho Golf Club before it got dark. 'All right – Mr Lattimer, Mr Sifuentes – draw closer, please.'

Arnie Becker watched the proceedings with a kind of fascinated awe. He had been in court perhaps more than a thousand times in his life, yet always as a disinterested player, instead of potential victim.

He saw the judge frowning while Sifuentes spoke; then turned to Lattimer, from the D.A.'s Office, and there followed an animated, almost angry exchange. Arnie could not quite hear what was being said; instead, he looked around the court for a glimpse of Lieutenant Saxby. He couldn't see him. Then the judge bawled out in a voice like a trucker's, 'Court will recess for ten minutes!'

15

From Russia With Aggro

Abby Perkins was working against the clock that Friday afternoon, trying to get off a letter to one of Arnie's clients, informing him that his wife had shipped his piano and four Chippendale chairs to Europe; as well as tying up some loose ends in Leland McKenzie's tray.

She had just filed a copy of the letter for Arnie, when the phone rang. She answered it with the machine crooked between her shoulder and chin. 'Yep – Abby Perkins.'

'*Abby is that you? I am here – I am hurt – I am going to the police . . . !*'

The voice filled Abby's warm heart with dread. 'Count Oblomov? What's happened? Where are you?'

The voice barked back. 'I have had a fight with that bastard Ross Hawkfoot' – he pronounced it 'Whorekveet' – 'and I am bloody well going to sue him for every cent he has!'

'Please, Count, tell me *where you are*?'

'I am in Emergency, at the Washington Hospital, and I am bleeding . . . !'

'Are you badly hurt?'

'I cannot speak to you now. I am in Emergency!' And the line went dead. Abby's neat little body collapsed in a chair and she almost wept. Then she remembered that it was *he* who had called *her*, yet he had been the one to cut her off. There was a lack of logic here somewhere – yet what did she expect?

She waited ten minutes for him to ring again, then looked at her watch. It wasn't far to the Washington Hospital, if she could find a cab. As for her work, she'd just have to take it home over the weekend.

Count Oblomov did not ring back. She decided to go

after him. It was probably futile; yet she also had awful visions of the Russian throwing himself off the tower of City Hall or wading out into the ocean with his pockets full of stones; and the long hysterical letter he'd leave – how his attorney, Abby Perkins, had abandoned him at the eleventh hour . . .

On her way out she looked into Brackman's office. He was labouring at a great mound of documents, and did not looked pleased to be disturbed. 'Yes, Abby?'

She said, 'Douglas, does the name Ross Hawkfoot mean anything to you?'

'Sure. He's Editor of the *Pacific Review* – one of the most respected liberal journals on the Coast. Why?'

'No – I just wondered. Thanks, Douglas.'

She got to the hospital at just before five o'clock. In Emergency it was still too early for the usual carnage of a Friday night – drunken fights, car smashes, battered wives, murders, O.D.'s. There was a merciful lull as Abby entered, breathing the sour metallic chill of the air-conditioning. Waiting their turn on the steel benches were a mother with two children, a girl in a mini-skirt who seemed to have broken her ankle, and a man with an eye injury.

To her huge relief there was no sign of her client. She went up to the desk and asked tentatively, 'Do you have a Count Oblomov here? He called me – said he was hurt.'

The clerk, a sleepy-looking Hispanic, pushed a big ledger at her; and to her dismay, she read, in a large florid handwriting, the legend: *COUNT YEVGENY MIKAILOVITCH OBLOMOV*. Instinctively, she looked for traces of blood on the page, as she pointed at the entry. 'Here – this one.'

'Name?'

She pointed again at the book. 'There – Count Oblomov!'

'*Your* name, lady.'

She wrote it down, in a column marked *Next of Kin*, and the clerk told her to wait. Abby was assailed by a conflict of emotions, none of them particularly uplifting. She was wasting precious time away from the office, and yet she was probably the only person in North America who'd be willing to minister to the Count in his hour of need.

She waited perhaps ten minutes, listening to the mewling of the child and the wail of ambulance sirens. Then a door opened, closed again with a *whooosh* and there emerged into the white surgical light an amazing figure, like a senile *Lawrence of Arabia*.

Count Oblomov was in a dressing-gown of vivid purple and crimson damask, embroidered Arab slippers, a thick towel round his neck, with traces of blood, a black eyepatch and a turban of bandages round his head. She could smell his rancid breath from several paces, as he bumped into the end of the bench, cursing in Russian. 'I can't see so good!' he roared.

She took him by the arm and led him outside where there was a cab rank. He showed neither surprise nor gratitude at her presence; but growled his address to the driver – a street in a not very salubrious area near Ladera Heights – while Abby tried to keep up a bold, business-like front.

'Count, tell me what happened?'

147

The Russian turned to her, his good eye glaring. '*Pas devant les domestiques!*' he hissed; then, when he saw she didn't fully understand, pointed to the back of the driver's head. 'Not here. These things are confidential!'

For the first time since she'd met him, Count Oblomov was almost entirely silent, until the cab pulled up outside a shabby wood-frame house on a steep hill. There were a couple of rusted cars at the kerb, both stripped of tyres and wheels. A group of Hispanic children were playing a game of tag. The evening air was grey and muggy. Count Oblomov leered at her. His lip had been cut and was now puffed up under a thick layer of antiseptic jelly. It did nothing for his appearance.

'My home from home!' he said, and got out, leaving Abby to pay the fare. Instead, she told the driver to wait. 'Count, I haven't got the time to come in. Why don't we make an appointment in the office on Monday?'

'Five minutes,' he said. 'All will be revealed.'

She made sure the cab driver would not leave her there, then followed the Russian up a steep flight of outside steps, up to a rickety wooden balcony lined with doors covered in wire mesh. Once, a long time ago, it had all been painted white; and even today some keen-eyed decorator might still have saved its period charm. But to Abby's eye the place seemed irredeemably squalid and depressing.

'I am only going to stay five minutes,' she said, like a girl out on her first tentative date.

Oblomov said nothing. He unlocked the frame door and bowed her in. There was just one large room – a

148

great cavern of a room, the like of which Abby had never seen before. Two of the walls, under a high ceiling, were covered in books; but these were not arranged on shelves, they were piled one upon the other, in tall precarious pillars. Some had subsided, even collapsed, so that half the floorspace was covered with books, loose or in jumbled heaps. Against the third wall, and under the window of the fourth, were stacked huge columns of newspapers, from which emanated a strange putrid smell, like a tomb.

The only furniture was a camp bed, unmade, a canvas chair and a cheap folding table on which stood an antique manual typewriter, of a kind that would have been out-of-date at the time of the Great Depression. There was no TV set, no radio. Through a door at the back Abby glimpsed an ice-box and the hint of a foul kitchen. She felt mildly alarmed, and wondered how she'd managed to get herself into this situation.

The Russian gave her his wolfish leer and disappeared through the door at the back, while Abby stood stock-still in the middle of the room. She noticed that most of the books on the floor were in Russian, as were the rotting newspapers.

Count Oblomov returned with two tumblers and a frosted bottle of Stolichnaya. He put them down on the table, after sweeping a pile of papers to the floor, and unscrewed the bottle. 'You try this, it is excellent. The best!'

'No. Please. Count, I can't stay long.'

As though not hearing her he poured out both glasses and offered one to her. She kept her hands at her side, noticing that there was only the one chair. The alternative would be the bed, from which she mentally and actually cringed.

'Tell me what happened?' she said again, praying that he would keep it short.

'I am going to sue the bastard Ross Whore-kveet for everything he is worth!' He swallowed half a tumber, gulped, steadied himself, then leered at her. *'Every bloody cent he has!'*

'But what did he *do*?' she asked, pleading.

'He insulted me! He humiliated me! He wanted to destroy me – destroy my work, destroy my mind, my precious creation . . . !'

'You wrote something for him – for his magazine?'

'Well of course! Why else would I deal with him? He is not a friend of mine – he is not, as we say, a man of culture. *Niey-kultuyny*. A vulgar bastard! You know what he wanted to do . . . ?' He was warming to his subject, pouring more vodka into his glass.

'No, do tell me,' she said, in a voice of near-despair.

'I translated for him a poem by Igor Livenshenko, one of the great dissidents of the Brezhnev era . . . You have heard of him, of course!'

'I'm sorry . . . ,' she murmured.

'He is magnificent – a mixture of Baudelaire and Swinburne. He committed suicide exactly twenty years ago. It was to mark the anniversary of his death that I translated one of his best poems – called *Fragments of Hell*. It is wonderful, terrific. You will find nothing in American literature to equal it!'

Abby, feeling the onset of panic, said, 'Just tell me what happened between you and this man Ross Hawkfoot?'

150

'Hawkfoot is, as you say, a low-down sonovabitch! That is the ABC of the matter! I spit in his grandfather's beard! That is all! *Finis! Koniec!*' And he ducked his mouth down and took another huge swallow from his glass.

'Count Oblomov, I really do have to get back to the office. Just tell me quickly what happened.'

'He rejected my translation. No, worse than that! Three months he has had it – *three bloody months!* – and then I go round to his office today in this great beautiful American building, with these beautiful secretaries sitting with their telephones and painted fingernails, like the whores of Babylon, and I demand to see the Editor – *Ross Hawkfoot Esquire!* I shouted his name, so there would be no misunderstanding. 'And you know what? You know what he did?'

'No, please tell me,' Abby said, trying to keep the alarm out of her voice.

'He did *nothing*! He hid in his office. Hid behind the whores with telephones, and absolutely refused to see me.' He paused, to pour himself another drink.

Abby said, tentatively: 'Count, did you have a contract with this editor, Hawksfoot? I mean, had he commissioned you to translate the poem?'

The Russian frowned and stuck a finger in his ear, working it round like some gardening implement. 'It was not so simple,' he said, his voice growing quieter, more circumspect. 'I met him at a party. At a literary salon – in Beverly Hills. He told me he was doing a big post-Glasnost article and I told him of all the poets I thought were good, and he said I must show him. He said to telephone him.'

151

He fixed Abby with his one bleak eye. 'So I telephoned him – I telephoned him every day – and always it was the same. One of the whores of Babylon told me he was busy or was not in the office. Finally, this morning, my patience with this *charade* ran out. I went round determined to confront him. I located his office and established that he was there inside. But at this point I encountered resistance. I was *attacked* by three women! I tell you, they were like tigresses!'

Abby listened, spellbound, while conceding a certain grudging respect for the Count. 'Were the three women the only ones to assault you?' she asked timidly.

'No. The bitches held me – both my arms and round the neck – while this Editor, this bloody Ross Hawkfoot, came out and started screaming for the police.' He suddenly paused, lowering his voice to a confidential whisper. 'You know, of course, that he is a homosexual?'

'I didn't know,' said Abby, truthfully.

'Aaah!' The Russian fixed her with his horrible, split-lipped grin. 'When he saw that I meant business, he went back into his office and came out with a glass coffee-machine. It was empty, otherwise I would have been scalded.'

'And he hit you?' she said, warming to the legal niceties.

'Well, first one of the women hit me with her shoe, then he hit me with his fist, then another of the whores hit me with *her* shoe, and it was then this bastard Ross hit me over the head with the coffee-machine!'

'How awful,' she said.

'Ahh! But I have not told you what *I did*!'

152

'No, tell me,' she said.

'I realised that the way of establishing good permanent relations with this literary barbarian – this lying pervert – so I decided to teach him a lesson. I broke free and grabbed the fire-extinguisher off the wall, banged it on the floor, then proceeded to spray the man *and the three whores*, until they were all covered in white foam. Like pillars of salt! It was magnificent!'

He congratulated himself by pouring himself yet another vodka which he downed in one, with a slow satisfied sigh. 'You have not drunk your glass, *chère Madame*,' he added, and his swollen glycerene lips curled into a dreadful grin, as he picked the second glass off the table and held it out to her. 'Please, drink!'

At this point Abby's nerve cracked. She turned, opened the door and looked over the balcony rail to make sure the cab was still there. It was. She went back and stood just inside the door. 'Shall I make an appointment for you to come to my office, Count?'

'When?'

'Tomorrow, in the afternoon. Four o'clock?' She was already making contingency plans for Michael Kuzak or Victor Sifuentes or, if necessary, both to stand in for her. 'Just one thing,' she added. 'You'll want to bring an action for assault?'

'Assault and bad faith. The second is perhaps more important.'

'I see.' She frowned. 'Did you do a lot of damage?'

'Tremendous damage!' He lifted his glass and drank an imaginary toast. 'The whole office looked as though it was covered in snow!'

'Yes, I see. Because it's possible, Count – even probable – that Ross Hawkfoot will want to bring charges against *you*.'

'Let him! Let him! We will smear his name from coast to coast. I shall even subpoena people from Russia to speak for Igor Livenshenko whose poem I translated. The case will become a literary *cause celebre*!'

She gave him her best artificial smile. 'I'll see you tomorrow then, at four o'clock.'

And even as she delivered the last phrase, she was already clattering on her high heels, along the terrace and down the dilapidated steps, to where the cab still stood, with the driver reading the sports page of *The Clarion*. She took a deep liberating breath of air, and gave the driver the address of the office.

16

Still Carrying a Torch

The judge called the court to order; he fixed first Arnie Becker, then Sifuentes, and finally Lattimer, from the D.A.'s Office, with a baleful stare.

'Mr Lattimer, I understand you have a statement to make to the court?'

'That is correct, your Honour.' Lattimer stood up and shot his cuffs, as he prepared to read from a pre-arranged text. 'In the People versus Arnold Becker, certain information has been received that has caused the District Attorney . . .'

'C'mon, c'mon, Mr Lattimer! This isn't the Supreme Court. Just tell us what you got to tell us.'

Lattimer took a deep breath, half turning to face the court. Arnie, watching him with thumping heart, noticed that not a hair of the man's bouffed and blow-dried style was out of place.

'The District Attorney's Office is not prepared to offer any evidence against Mr Becker. I therefore submit that he go free.'

'I so direct,' the judge said, as Becker and Sifuentes slapped each other's shoulders. 'However, there are certain points,' he went on, 'that I'd like to have entered into the record.'

Becker felt Sifuentes' hand stiffen on his arm. Statements from the Bench were just the thing to have the reporters scribbling in their little books.

'As I understand it,' the judge continued, in his ominous growl, 'it was the intention of the police to produce a packet which allegedly contained cocaine, which which *allegedly* was found on the defendant Mr Becker's person.'

He paused here, with his slow stare enveloping all

three attorneys below him. 'I must emphasise that Mr Becker here, who is a man of exemplary character, has protested his innocence from the moment he was arrested at a beach party in Santa Monica a few days ago. Mr Becker is a professional man with a considerable reputation to lose. However, being also a prudent man and knowing that his reputation was on the line, Mr Becker had an independent analysis made of the packet. This analysis showed that it contained a harmless substance which *looked* like cocaine. There were also two sets of fingerprints on the packet. Neither of these belonged to the defendant.

'In dismissing this case,' he went on, 'I call upon the senior police officer in charge, Lieutenant Dwight Saxby, to provide this court with a full and frank disclosure of how he thinks this near-tragedy came about. I should add that I shall be passing his statement on to his superior officer, together with any appropriate comments I deem necessary. Mr Becker, you may go.'

As Sifuentes hurried Becker out through the side door, they both caught a glimpse of Lieutenant Saxby, his face puffed and dark with rage. He saw Becker and Sifuentes in the same instant, and seemed for a moment undecided as to whether he should confront them both or explode. Just then Sifuentes made up his mind for him. He strode up to the lieutenant and started speaking to him, and as he did so, the man's face turned a strange unnatural colour – from dark puce to a sickly bluish-grey, so that Becker feared he might be having a seizure.

Sifuentes came striding back, with a grin of satisfaction. 'That bastard's not going to sleep too well in the next few nights.'

'What did you say to him? He looks as sick as a parrot.'

'I told him we were going to charge him with wrongful arrest, wrongful imprisonment, and gross violation of your Constitutional Rights. But what really got to him was when I said we were sending the fingerprints to the D.A.'s Office, with instructions to have his own prints tested. He didn't like that. So he called me a wop – to which I replied I'm not a wop – I'm a Spaniard, with a touch of Moorish.'

Just then Arnie Becker saw a pretty blonde woman in a grey dress-for-success suit crossing the lobby with a black briefcase. Becker grabbed Sifuentes' arm. 'There's Grace . . . !' He smiled, and as he started after her, called, 'Thanks, buddy. Have a nice day!'

He caught up with her in the main hall outside the courts. 'Grace!'

She turned. 'Arnie! How nice.'

'Could you do with a drink?'

She hesitated. 'Well-ll-ll . . .'

'That means Yes.'

'What means Yes?'

'Hesitation. Hesitation in a woman always means Yes.'

'I see.' She looked tired and slightly tense. 'Okay. But you know, do you, that I don't drink?'

'Ahh.' He nodded, remembering somewhere that she'd sworn never to drink again. It had somehow been tied up with her relationship with Michael Kuzak. 'The Tamberlain Café all right?' he asked her.

159

'Fine.' And she began to lead the way towards the entrance. Halfway – as Becker should have known – they were accosted by two reporters.

'Any comment on what the judge said, Mr Becker . . . ?'

'How d'you think this case is gonna affect your standing as a leading attorney in this city, Mr Becker?'

'There *was* no case!' Becker said angrily. 'The judge threw it out. Weren't you fellas in court?'

'We was hanging around to see if Calvados showed up again . . .'

Grace van Owen had stopped and was listening. 'Arnie?'

He turned to her his most winning smile. 'Don't worry – I had a spot of trouble – bent cop planted what looked like cocaine in my pocket.'

The two journalists started gabbling together. 'You say a *bent* cop, Mr Becker?'

'May I quote you on that, Mr Becker?'

A flash went off very near his face. He turned and yelled, 'You quote anything and I'll see Lieutenant Saxby sues you both in person. Now you guys, *be missing*!' He took Grace's arm and marched her through the big doors and down the steps to the street below.

'You shouldn't have been so rude to them,' she said. 'It never pays. Those guys have got more power than we have. We have to abide by a very rigid set of rules. Those guys just make up the rules as they go along.'

They found a table half-draped in the statutory baby-palm in a tub. A girl came and said, 'Hi you guys! What'll it be?'

He ordered milkshakes, vanilla, for two. 'At least

there's one sane woman left in the State of California.'

'Meaning?'

'You don't spend your whole life worrying about your figure. Which, incidentally,' he said, with his shark-toothed smile, 'is very nice indeed.'

'Oh I worry all right, Arnie. Only I worry about other things.'

'Such as?'

'Oh, the usual things. Getting old. Living alone. Wondering if I'll spend my whole life lawyering, with nothing to show at the end of it, except grey hair and a crocodile skin handbag for a face. No husband, no children . . .'

Her face seemed suddenly on the brink of collapse: her mouth drooped, her eyes grew heavy with unshed tears. He took her hand in his, and squeezed it. 'Do you want to talk about it?'

'Not much. I mean, it wouldn't do any good, would it?'

'Well – we could try. My place or yours?'

She suddenly threw back her head and gave a bleak laugh. 'Arnold Becker, you are actually trying to seduce me! I've heard about the famous Becker charm, only I never thought it would be so unsubtle!'

Becker shrugged. 'You're very attractive, Grace. I've always thought so.'

She smiled. 'Well . . . I'm flattered, I guess. And it's nice of you, Arnie, but . . .'

'You still carrying a torch for Mike Kuzak?'

Her face flushed all the way down to her neckline, and her expression was tense, miserable. 'How is Michael?' she said, very quietly.

161

'Same as ever, I guess. What do you want to know?'

'Does he' – her voice had thickened into a hoarse whisper, as she leant close to Becker – 'is he in a relationship just now?'

'Well –' He paused, noting the anguish in her eyes, knowing she was terrified of the answer.

Becker made an empty gesture, palms up. 'The honest truth, Grace, is I don't know.'

'Ah c'mon, Arnie, don't give me that old lawyer's bullshit. Who's Mike screwing?'

'I don't know. Honest. Maybe no-one.'

The waitress brought their milkshakes and Becker paid. He somehow didn't think this was going to be a very long conversation.

She stared at her glass and her face was full of a deep, lonely sadness. It was nothing sudden or transitory, but an expression of something that had matured from within, and which might mark her beautiful face forever.

Becker had the feeling that he was intruding on private grief. He said, 'Look, Grace, I have a very great respect for you. We all do at McKenzie Brackman. But I feel I've handled this all wrong –'

'Not at all. If I'd been in the mood, your approach would have worked just dandy!'

He smiled. The sadness and the power-dressing were a potent combination. But she was still in love with someone else, so what the hell. His pride was also dented by the fact that she had not once asked him about the reporters' questions. In fact, he realised now that she had only agreed to come out for a drink in order to question him about Kuzak. Speak about 'unsubtle approaches'.

162

He stood up and held out his hand. 'Good to see you again, Grace.'

She gave him a brave smile. 'Arnie – don't say anything to Mike.'

'I'm a divorce lawyer, Grace. I know how to keep secrets, if nothing else.'

'I know, Arnie. I'm sorry – it's just that I'm a little tired today.'

At the entrance he turned and looked at her. She hadn't moved a muscle and her eyes were fixed on some faraway point beyond the horizon.

17

Gonzales Watches Her Tail

Abby burst into the office, out of breath, her hair mildly dishevelled. She ran up to Roxanne. 'Oh God am I glad to be back!'

Sifuentes strolled over with a cup of iced water. 'Hello Abby. Have fun with the Prince?'

'He's not a Prince. I'm not even sure he's a Count.' She gave Sifuentes a plaintive smile. 'I just don't know what I've let myself in for. Or rather, I *do* know, and it's a mess!'

'Take it easy,' said Roxanne. 'Just tell us.'

Abby told them the whole sequence of events that afternoon, and when she told them about the Russian being attacked by three women simultaneously, plus the esteemed editor of the *Pacific Review*, and had responded by drenching them all with fire extinguisher foam, Roxanne and Sifuentes started to laugh. They laughed and laughed.

'Oh wonderful, Abby!' Sifuentes cried. 'It's even better than that case I did of the Professor having his wig lifted off on TV. If it comes to court, Abby, you'd better have some lock-jaw surgery to stop you laughing!'

'I happen not to think it very funny,' she said primly.

'Well, that's fine. You can defend your Russian with a completely straight face.'

'Victor, I think you're patronising me.'

'Abby, Abby, Abby!' he cried; but she was already walking quickly away towards her office. Sifuentes turned to Roxanne, with a broad gesture of resignation. 'See what happens when Old Man McKenzie goes sick. Stuart and Ann Kelsey are on the point of no return, I have to snatch Arnie from the jaws of eternal ignomy,

Abby gets saddled with a nutcase, and Brackman starts prowling about the office like an FBI man with not enough to do.'

'So what are *you* doing now?' Roxanne asked.

Sifuentes told her about the triumph in court that afternoon. 'Case of police corruption,' he said, 'always sticks in my throat. Can't absolutely prove it, can't absolutely disprove it.'

'By the way,' Roxanne said. 'Where is Arnie?'

'I left him talking to Grace Van Owen. We bumped into her at the courthouse. Why?'

'Oh, it's something to do with the Gloria Gonzales case. It's highly confidential – for obvious reasons – but he had me hire a private investigator and I've got their first report right here.'

'Anything nice and salacious?'

'Victor! You know I wouldn't dream of reading confidential documents for the firm!' She sounded genuinely shocked at the idea.

'Oh well, I expect he'll be in soon. But you know what Arnie is – always a bit of a loner. Indoor-man and nightbird. Does that sum him up?'

Roxanne laughed. 'No! That's the way he'd *like* us to see him. I mean, you can imagine a really seasoned *roué* allowing himself to go on a blind date, and not noticing that all the other guests are doped out of their skull! Arnie's an innocent, Victor!'

'I guess so. But at least he's off the hook. But what are we going to do about Abby?'

'You must get someone to take over her case,' said Roxanne. 'It's not that she's out of her depth. She's absolutely terrified.'

'But the Count's an old man, for Chrissake!'

'According to her, that makes it even worse. She says he's a violent, drunken lunatic. I think someone should play the white knight and take over.'

'Okay, Roxanne. The hint is taken. I'll have a little chat with her.'

*

The show was into its last minutes and most of the participants and audience were beginning to sweat under the banks of blinding studio lights. Only Gloria Gonzales appeared to be cool, with a controlled passion and energy that fired the programme and attracted more than twenty million viewers from coast to coast.

The secret of the show was simple. On the premise that almost nobody, from whatever walk of life, will deliberately choose *not* to go on national TV, Gloria Gonzales homed in on every category of misfortune and tragedy, whether self-inflicted, accidental or as a result of what the insurance companies call an Act of God.

Over the last few years her show had chalked up vivid, sometimes melodramatic confrontations, covering topics that ranged from rape, murder, incest, infidelity, wife battering, homosexuality, lesbianism, sado-masochism, child-abuse, AIDS, alcoholism, depression, suicide, over-eating, and, of course, drug-addiction.

This was one of Gloria's favourites – so much so that she'd tackled it twice already. She liked it because there were clear villains (pushers) and victims (users), while combining the two essentials of Greek tragedy, pity and terror, with the twin Californian obsessions of neurotic guilt and public self-exposure, leading to a state of frozen hysteria.

From time to time her producers murmured that something was a 'down' subject, a turn-off, or the advertisers would get nervous; but she countered by claiming that she performed a social need – a claim that was invariably made at well-attended press conferences – and so powerful were her name and her ratings, that any doubts were quickly squashed.

Meanwhile, the reputation of Ms Gloria Gonzales as a force for good in the land remained intact. Those who disliked Gloria Gonzales – and there were many – tended to be intellectuals and purists, and for them she had a ready pre-packed argument: were these pointy-heads trying to say that such evils as alcoholism or child-abuse should not be discussed – not even mentioned? Did these intellectuals not care about the sad, lonely, derelict people who had fallen through the safety-net of the Great Society . . . ?

But for one who was prepared to strip her victims of every layer of emotion, Ms Gloria Gonzales had an astonishingly thin skin when it came to criticism of herself. She employed a full-time cuttings agency to scour every newspaper and magazine in the country; and also to record every reference to her on national TV and radio. If there was any transgression she sued. But her regular lawyers were experts only in the game of libel and slander. Which is why she'd come to Arnie Becker for her divorce. As she said, Horses for Courses.

The floor manager was making winding-up signs. Gloria was comforting a man who had just turned in his 17-year-old son to the police. He had found the boy with half an ounce of hashish in his pocket. The man was weeping uncontrollably on to Gloria's semi-naked shoulder and she could feel the tepid tears seeping down under her plunge-line dress of rough, sapphire-coloured Thai silk. 'There you go, honey, just let it out, *let it out* . . . !' – while her earpiece crackled with the producer's voice. 'Have it tie it up there, Gloria – long shot – and hold – *nice, nice* . . . !'

The cameras off. Gloria brusquely disengaged herself from the blubbing little man on her shoulder, crossed the studio floor at a fair clip, and disappeared into her dressing-room where she poured herself a generous glass of whisky. 'Rossata!'

'Yes, ma'am?'

'Get Mr Clay. At once.'

The timid little Columbian girl bowed, said, 'Yes ma'am!' and withdrew.

Gloria Gonzales sat in front of the mirror, under the brutal overhead lighting, and inspected the tiny spreading mosaic of lines and creases that not even the most expensive facial treatment in Beverly Hills could entirely eradicate.

There was a light knock on the door and a small spry man in a tight-fitting double-breasted suit slid in with a little smile. 'Hi Gloria. Great show!'

'Have they found that snooper yet?'

'Well, to tell you the truth –'

'That's exactly what I want you to tell me!'

'Well, I'm afraid I checked everything out – had a

word with Security – but nobody seems to have seen anything.'

'Then they didn't look hard enough! I tell you, I've had a tail on me for at least two days now.'

'Well, I'm sorry, Gloria but it just doesn't look –'

'You trying to tell me I'm getting paranoid, is that it?'

'No, Gloria. I'm just saying you're mistaken.'

'Look, I've got a feel about these things. You're in the public eye and you make enemies. For instance, tonight – the drug barons. You don't know what you're taking on. Then there are the psychos, the sex fiends. You think I like going back home and knowing that every nut-'n-fruitcake out there is maybe planning to break in?'

Rollo Clay stood with hands politely clasped, and looked concerned. 'I'm sure if you're still worried, Security could lay on something.'

She considered this for a moment, then frowned and said, 'I'll think about it. And by the way, that boy tonight who claims he was framed by the cops on a drug-rap – drop it.'

'But I thought you promised him?'

'Didn't you hear – *drop it*! It's the corniest gag in the book. That'll be all, Rollo.'

'Goodnight, Gloria.'

She waited till the door closed, then quickly dialled a number. While she waited she instinctively put a hand over the mouthpiece, as though there might be eavesdroppers in the room.

'Darling?' She spoke in a hoarse whisper. 'I know, but I had to call you. We've got a peeper . . . No, I'm still at the studio. Don't call me at home in case it's bugged . . . No, darling, I don't. Love you . . . night . . . !'

She put down the phone and sank into the chair in front of the mirror, her face a powdered mask of worry and rage.

*

Arnie Becker got back to the office at the end of the afternoon. He didn't smell of booze and he didn't tell everyone that he'd tried unsuccessfully to get a date with Grace Van Owen.

Douglas Brackman was off the prowl for the moment. His hands were full trying to get an actor off a charge of sending a Head of Studio over one thousand unwanted items by mail-order, including fifty outsize mint-green women's dresses and one hundred copies of *American Psycho* from a book club.

To pile it on, the actor was countersuing, in the civil court, the Head of Studio for bad-mouthing him all round Hollywood, so that he was now getting no work. It was Brackman's task, among others, to prove that he was a good actor in the first place. Not easy.

Roxanne leapt up and gave Arnie a big hug as he came in. 'I heard, from Victor – it's wonderful!'

'You should have heard the judge. He sure put it on the line with that cop. By the way, how's Leland?'

She shrugged. 'Well, you know – takes time. Oh by the way, I got the first report' – she lowered her voice – 'from Sherwoods, the Private Investigator people.'

She handed him the stiff brown envelope, sent by Special Courier, with a red sticker: *PHOTOGRAPHS. DO NOT BEND* – it was sealed at both ends with double-strength adhesive tape.

'Thanks, honey. Seems kinda funny being a free man again!'

'Good luck, Arnie.'

In his office was the usual pile of mail that collected every day like driftwood on a beach. Roxanne usually weeded out what was not important – the junk mail and the cranks – but passed on everything else, including letters from angry or embittered ex-clients, even threats from ex-spouses, which he'd learnt could not just be thrown in the trash can.

This afternoon, however, he decided that the stack of envelopes could keep till tomorrow. The Sherwood File would be plenty to be getting on with. He slit one end with his pocket-knife and slid out about two dozen glossy 10" by 12" black and white prints, and about a dozen in colour. There was also a covering letter from Sherwoods, plus a detailed breakdown of the hours spent on the case, with venues and times, as well as relevant comments on the subject's movements.

As soon as he started riffling through the photographs, he knew that something was wrong. He turned to the covering letter, enclosing an invoice for seven days' work – $5,850, expenses included. He pressed the intercom. 'Roxanne, it's Arnie. Could you drop by a moment. It's important.'

She was with him in less than twenty seconds, giving him her cheerful, buxom smile.

He held the covering letter from Sherwoods in his

hand. 'Rox, when I asked you to get a P.I. for the Gloria Gonzales divorce case, what exact instructions did you give?'

The smile had faded. She looked worried. 'Well – I called them first. Spoke to someone called Rooney.'

'That's right – Ted Rooney – ex-detective with the L.A.P.D. What did you say to him?'

Her lip trembled. 'I told him . . . I told him . . . Oh my God!'

Arnie nodded grimly 'You were supposed to get a tail put on the husband. Instead, you put it on Gloria Gonzales. Honey, if she finds out, this could cost McKenzie Brackman a pretty penny!'

She broke down, weeping almost hysterically. 'Oh my God! Oh my God! It was just that everything was so chaotic, with Leland being in hospital and you having to worry about that dreadful case . . . !'

While she'd been speaking, he had once more been going through the stack of prints. He now held up his hand. 'I accept responsibility, Roxanne. It's my case and I should have handled it personally. P.I. work is always a very delicate business. If it goes wrong it can have catastrophic results.' She sobbed again, even louder than before.

'It's okay, honey. It's *okay*. Because as it happens, I think you may have turned up something very useful. All I ask is that you keep absolutely quiet about what's happened.'

'I'd hardly tell everyone in the office! Oh, Arnie, I'm so ashamed!'

'It's okay, honey. Just between you and me – huh?'

'Absolutely,' she said, sniffing.

175

He turned back to the photos. 'Just one other thing – could you make me some strong black coffee?'

'With no sugar? Right away, sir!'

*

The TV News gave Arnie's acquittal a nice thirty-second spot, showing him smiling outside the court, followed by the judge's savage indictment of Lieutenant Saxby, who was filmed looking as though he'd just swallowed a bucketful of cement.

Arnie was particularly bucked, because Leland had seen it too, and while he was usually not happy about gratuitous publicity for the firm, he was nevertheless pleased that one of his team had come out on top.

But Arnie had not been counting on Gloria Gonzales. The *Clarion* that morning had quite a splash, putting the knife into Saxby and the L.A.P.D. with a vengeance. But while Arnie Becker was portrayed as a victim of probable police corruption, he was also described as '*the playboy divorce-lawyer of the rich and famous . . . one of L.A.'s most eligible bachelors . . . Unfaithful wives will no doubt be standing in line to win his favours and get shot of their dull old husbands . . .*'

'Gee-whizz, Arnie, you're famous,' Kuzak said, as they met in the lift that morning.

Becker shrugged. 'I suppose I'd better go and see Leland. He can be tricky about publicity.'

'Oh he'll be okay. He's probably relieved you're not gonna spend a couple of months in the slammer.'

'Thanks, Mike! And how are you fixed?'

'I've taken on Abby's mad Russian. D'you know how

176

old that guy is? Sixty-nine years old, and he sprays the editor of the Pacific Review with fire-extinguishing foam! It's going to make a lovely story.'

As they both entered the office, smiling at Roxanne, the long solemn face of Douglas Brackman peered at them along the corridor. 'Arnie – a word.'

Arnie Becker entered Brackman's office, refreshed from the first good night's sleep he'd had in days, and full of confidence.

'Sit down,' said Brackman. 'I've had your client on the phone.'

'Which one?'

'Gloria Gonzales – the fearless crusader for the underprivileged, for the victims of the Affluent Society. Who stands up for cripples and perverts and addicts, and all that's most deserving of pity . . .'

'You get that from her or you make it up?' Arnie said, grinning.

'Ah don't get fresh with me, Arnie. If something goes wrong in this office – while Leland's away – *I'm* the one that carries the can.'

'Okay. So what's Miss Gonzales been saying?'

'She says she hired you on the understanding that there would be no further publicity concerning you.'

'Well, there's publicity, and there's publicity. I'd say that getting a clean bill of health on a drug rap would be just her thing.'

'Well, you got it wrong. The lady says you promised her, when she asked you to handle her divorce, that there would be *no further publicity*. Is that right?'

'Yeah, well . . . Look, Douglas, the woman's a megalomaniac! She comes in here and starts laying

177

down the ground rules – I mean, she's in the publicity game – she knows that you can't always control what appears in the media. Even *she* can't!'

'Well, she was on the phone this morning – three calls before nine o'clock. She says she retained you in the strictest confidence, on the understanding that you keep your name out of the papers.'

'So what am I supposed to do? Buy up all the remaining stock of today's *Clarion* and have 'em pulped?'

Brackman stared at him gloomily across the table. 'She wants to talk to you personally at eleven. You'd better be ready.'

'I'll wear my flak-vest and groin-protector,' he said.

18

Markowitz Meets
His Moll

Stuart Markowitz was sunk in the deepest slough of despond. He had ensconced himself in the Napoleon Bonaparte Suite at the top of the Berlimont Hotel, with a balcony on two sides overlooking both the ocean and the mountains, leaving the city under a brown haze far below.

It was his second night at the hotel. He left at eight in the morning, by chauffeur-driven limousine, in time to arrive early at the office. And he left again, in the same limo, at six, returning straight to the hotel. He'd only seen his wife once since leaving their home, and that was a quick glimpse as she was heading for morning conference and he was going to the lavatory. It was an embarrassing, even demeaning incident. He had not himself been attending conference because his time was almost completely absorbed with the lovely Emily Stallwood's husband's affairs.

This morning he decided not to go into the office at all. He had brought two boxes of documents to the hotel, which would take at least twenty-four hours to unravel. A lot of the work could be done on the telephone, to contacts he had in law firms and banks in New York, London and Geneva. He was determined to immerse himself in the intricacies of Marcus Stallwood's finances. At least, it would keep him from thinking of Ann.

A WASP, that's what she was – a White Anglo-Saxon Protestant – while he was the bright little Israelite, the tax wizard, the self-effacing lawyer who had twice brought Emily Stallwood expensive lunches, and who now stood wrongly accused of adultery. No victim of the McCarthy witchhunt in the fifties could have felt more helpless, more desperate than did Stuart Markowitz in this hour of travail.

He had breakfasted on one cup of tea and half a grapefruit. He stared mournfully across the sitting-room, into the bedroom. The suite seemed enormous, desolate. He could feel the tears itching at the back of his eyes. His nose twitched. He was making some headway. Marcus Stallwood had assets in five different countries, including Hong Kong. So far Stuart had detected at least three gross violations of the Internal Revenue Service's rules. If Stuart were not of such a timid temperament, he had more than enough with which to blackmail Emily's husband till the turn of the century.

He played with the idea, but never seriously. He might mention it to her over lunch. They were due to have lunch again today. He would make it an occasion. *The Trianon* set just the right tone: soft candelabra, linen tablecloths, and plenty of space between the tables. He picked up the phone and dialled her number; then suddenly pressed down the bar to cut himself off. He was not a particularly God-fearing man, but he knew that in some religions it is enough to have *contemplated* a deadly sin, to have put oneself on the wrong side of God. Was adultery – even thinking of adultery – worse than mere blackmail? he wondered. Supposing he committed both?

But this was crazy. He was a lawyer – a very expensive lawyer – and this was the sort of advice that ordinary mortals had to pay hundreds of dollars an hour to receive. He looked at his watch. Just after eleven. That gave him one hour – or ninety minutes at the outside – to tackle London again. He'd get back to Geneva tomorrow morning, with an alarm call at five-thirty.

'Hello, James Roxburgh speaking' – the honeyed English vowels were full of self-confidence, and just a trace of arrogance – 'Ah Stuart, yes, I've been waiting for you to call.' A slight hesitation. 'Is this line secure?'

Stuart Markowitz felt his heart miss a beat. 'I think we can chance it?'

'Ye-es, well as a matter of fact, we decided to part company with your friend about six months ago. In other words, we suggested that he withdraw all his investments.'

'Why?'

'Well' – he cleared his throat with a genteel cough – 'I take it you will understand that as an institution of some repute, we have to be absolutely happy with the money we handle.' Another studied pause. 'In the case of this particular depositor, suffice it to say that we were not entirely happy with the *provenance* of the money, and the fact that so much of it was in very large amounts of cash.' Pause. 'Hello? You still there, Stuart?'

Stuart swallowed, and found that his mouth was as dry as sandpaper. 'Thank you, James. I think I've got the picture.'

'Well I'm glad to be of help. Just one thing. I'd give this character a wide berth, if I was you.'

Stuart gulped, thanked him, and hung up. His palms were quite damp. Oh my God, what have I let myself in for? I've lost my wife, and now I'm involved with the Mob.

*

Roxanne took the call, then tiptoed into Becker's office to tell him face to face. 'Arnie? – it's Gloria Gonzales. D'you want me to talk to her? Or would you like me to put her off?'

'Why should I? She's a client, isn't she?'

'Mmm. I just thought on your first day back – after the hearing . . .'

'Stop mothering me, Roxanne! Put the woman on!'

Thirty seconds later the phone purred and he picked it up and said, in a voice like warm maple syrup: 'Arnold Becker speaking.'

'Becker?' Her tone was neutral-to-hard. 'I want to see you right away.'

'This morning?'

'At the Polo Lounge, Beverly Hills Hotel, at noon.'

He mimed the time it took to turn the page of his appointments book, which had become ominously empty since the busted beach party. 'Now let me see,' he began, wanting to sound busy but relaxed. 'This morning –'

'This morning you're seeing me! I suggest you scrap your other appointments.'

For a moment Becker sat chewing the knuckle of one finger, sorely tempted to tell the woman to go boil her head in the microwave. He glanced at the plain brown envelope from the Sherwood P.I. agency, noticed it was just past eleven o'clock, and said into the phone, 'I'll try to make it as near noon as I can. But I have to make some calls first.'

'I'll see you there,' she said, and hung up.

Becker put the Sherwood envelope in his Samsonite attaché case, making sure it was locked, then went out and leaned over close to Roxanne so she could smell his Paco Rabanne aftershave. 'I'm off to the Polo Lounge at the Beverly Hills Hotel,' he murmured, like a conspirator.

'Mmmm! is this to be a tryst with Miss Gonzales? Should I be jealous?'

'No, honey-baby, I'm keeping myself all for you. You know where I'll be – and if I'm not back by sundown send out the First Cav!' He gave her an Indian salute. 'I'll get a cab in the street.'

He arrived outside the Beverly Hills Hotel with a few minutes to spare. Unlike most places in L.A., it didn't try too hard. It didn't have to. Although connoisseurs might argue as to whether it was the best hotel in the world, it was generally agreed that it was one of the most famous. Which was another way of saying that you always saw famous people there.

Arnie Becker went through into the Polo Lounge, which looked as though it had been recently refurbished by Mussolini for Marie Antoinette. Among the pre-prandial guests, Arnie spotted Jane Fonda, a Pulitzer Prize-winning novelist, and a little bald man with spectacles who was Hollywood's top agent, nicknamed the King Cobra, and feared and loathed accordingly.

Waiters and *maitre-d's* glided among the tables like courtiers. One of them appeared at Arnie's elbow, and as soon as the name Gonzales was spoken, he was led directly to a small table in an alcove, behind some rich, exotic flora and as nearly private as a table in a Hollywood hotel *can* be private.

Arnie ordered a Campari soda and made sure his

case was well concealed under the table, where he could feel it resting against his ankle. Then, with some pleasure, he transgressed one of Hollywood's most tiresome taboos: he lit one of his oval-shaped, gold-tipped Abdullah No. 5 cigarettes which he had sent to him from Bond Street, London. So, relaxed in his Italian silk suit and blue polka-dot silk tie, one of L.A.'s most formidable divorce lawyers sat in wait for one of L.A.'s most powerful and dangerous women.

*

When Stuart Markowitz stepped in to the Trianon Restaurant on Wilshire – reputed to be, if not the best restaurant in town, certainly the most expensive – he already felt like an adulterer. He had a champagne cocktail to start with, then sat busily studying the handwritten menu, if only to avoid eye-contact with any of the other guests. Supposing one of Ann Kelsey's friends walked in? *Or Ann herself?* The thought made him feel slightly sick.

When Mrs Stallwood arrived he experienced a mixture of stage fright and exhilaration, charged with another underlying emotion which he diagnosed, with some alarm, as sexual attraction.

'Emily, my dear!' He stood up and made room for her, relieved to be sitting down again because it disguised the marked difference in their heights.

Emily Stallwood was dressed in a sort of kaftan of finely spun, burnt sienna wool. She wore a diamond ring, but no wedding ring; and her rich amber hair flowed down over her shoulders like a Pre-Raphaelite painting. She also ordered a champagne cocktail.

They small talked for a few minutes, and the waiter took their orders for Beluga caviar, baked pheasant and green salad; and, with studied nonchalance, Stuart ordered a bottle of the Krug '74.

'You're spoiling me!' she said, smiling through her eyelashes; and Stuart was uncomfortably aware of her long warm body under the thin, loose wool. He found himself wondering if she were wearing any underwear; and in the turmoil of his mind he ordered two more cocktails.

'Are you trying to get me drunk?' she said. 'Wearing down my resistance?'

He gave a nervous laugh that was more like a hiccough. 'I assumed this was strictly business?' he said.

'Business with pleasure, I hope?' She had finished her first cocktail; as soon as the second glass arrived, she downed half of it in one gulp. She seemed to have a thirst like an Australian bush-whacker.

'I like you, Stuart. I like you because you're nice and cosy and understanding. And I like you because I just *hate* my husband. Marcus. *Marcus!* Who does he think he is with a name like that – a Roman centurion?' She giggled and ducked her lips down to her nearly empty glass.

Stuart chose this turn of the conversation, such as it was, to broach with her something that had been worrying him increasingly all morning. 'Emily, would you mind if I asked you what your husband does?'

She looked at him very directly. 'Well he doesn't screw me, that's for sure.'

187

He blushed, not knowing quite whether she intended this as an invitation to her bed. This time the very thought made him feel giddy, and he could feel his heart pounding – knowing this was the very worst thing for his health. The doctors would go crazy. And Ann . . . The thought of her was even worse. The champagne arrived, and when their glasses were full, he tried again. 'Emily, I want you to understand that you can talk to me in absolute confidence. I'm like a priest, or a doctor. You can trust me.'

'Well I should darn well hope so, after all you've told me about my beloved husband's little piggy banks all over the world!'

'Yes, well that's just the point, Emily. You see, I understand that your husband runs a finance house, in the Caymans, that deals in a large number of commodities, and that these are channelled through a lot of different banks in different countries.'

'Yeah, well that's what I told you at our first meeting. Is that all you've managed to find out in the last month?'

'Well, not exactly.' He chose his words with care, pausing while the waiter poured the champagne. 'You told me he doesn't keep much cash in the States – just enough fast money to keep him going?'

'Yeah, that's right.'

'You know he has a twenty per cent share in a hotel in Vegas?'

'Yeah, but he said I'd never get my hands on that, or I'd finish up' – she took a deep swig of champagne – 'I'd finish feeding the sharks off Tampona Point.'

'Your husband certainly doesn't sound a very nice man,' Stuart said, wondering whether she was dumb, or just playing dumb.

19

Rattlesnake in a
Beehive

A blood-red Rolls-Royce Corniche, with wine-red leather upholstery and smoked windows, drew up outside the Beverly Hills Hotel with a sound like falling leaves. A black chauffeur with white gloves held open the door and the Queen of Chat Shows stepped out, wrapped in a Russian sable. She was followed by two large young men, scrubbed and trim, like college football players, each carrying a two-way pocket radio.

Inside the Polo Lounge, so used to the rich and famous, her arrival nevertheless caused the kind of breathless hush that is usually reserved for visiting Heads of State. In order to reach Becker's table in the far corner, she had to cross the room diagonally, while her two minders fanned out on either side, like Secret Servicemen.

Two flunkeys drifted round her, smirking with adoration. Becker noted that she was twenty minutes late, as he half stood up, squashing out his third Turkish cigarette.

She marched up to his table, glared at him, then produced from under the sable wrap a small recording device which she placed on the table between them. Arnie saw that the tiny red recording light was on. He grinned. 'That thing for my benefit, Gloria – or just for posterity?'

A flunkey hovered, asking her what she wanted to drink, but she waved him away. Becker ordered another Campari.

She sat down opposite him. 'I'll have you know, Mr Becker, that I'm not in a very nice mood today. I'm very near to getting mad – and when I get mad, I get mean!'

He studied her for a moment: this goddess of the cathode-tube, Grand Inquisitor of the little screen, this creature of whom it was claimed that she influenced and manipulated more Americans than the State Governor, or any number of Senators and Congressmen, perhaps even more than the President himself.

Here was brute egomania in the flesh, Arnie thought; and looking at her now, even in the gentle hotel lighting, he marvelled again at how extraordinarily unsexy she was. Her hair and skin and teeth and lips had a shiny artificial quality, as though moulded from various textures of plastic, like some life-size doll. Even her black skin-clinging business suit seemed to accentuate the angles of her body, rather than the curves; and her shoes looked like lethal weapons.

Arnie had decided to take his time. Like Sid Field and Jack Benny, he thought, it was all in the timing.

'So am I to understand that I'm out of favour?' His tone was neutral, but the mocking irony implicit.

'You know damn well you are! I spoke to your Mr Brackman first thing this morning, after I seen the papers. I must say, I'm a little surprised he's not here now.'

Arnie shrugged. 'He didn't mention anything to me. Why didn't you arrange for us both to meet in his office? I'm sure he'd have found the time.'

'Don't be so goddamned patronising to me, Mr Becker!' she yelled – and it was no longer the tough but controlled voice of America's First Lady of TV; it was now the pure *barrio* of Mexico City, rendered into an unlovely North American snarl.

'You think you're a fancy lawyer so you can play the

194

big-shot with me!' Her eyes were two points of black fire. 'I retained you for good money, because I heard you were the best – the *best*! – *Hijo de puta!* – so what the hell can all the other goddam lawyers be like in this city of crooks and clowns and con-artists!' She was shouting now, giving half the Polo Lounge the benefit of her views on Arnie Becker, L.A. divorce lawyer.

She goes on like this, he thought, and she's going to be looking at a writ for slander and gross defamation of character. He could walk out, of course, but that would mean surrendering in front of *le tout monde* of L.A. society. Besides, that was probably just what she wanted.

He nodded, smiling with admiration. 'I congratulate you, Miss Gonzales, for an excellent grasp of rhetoric. I doubt I can match it. So' – he leaned back, fingers steepled together – 'How can I help you?'

Her black eyes now bulged with rage, and her jaw muscles contracted under her tight skin like the moving of some reptile. He watched her, fascinated and repelled.

'You'd better start thinking about helping yourself!' she hissed. 'We had a deal. It was a good deal. It was goddam generous, because I coulda kicked your ass instead. You were in trouble!' Her voice rose menacingly. 'You had a drug rap hanging over you! But I was nice about it. I said okay – as long as there's *no more publicity*. Then I look in the paper today and you're all over the front page, and some snooper's written that you're even working for me! How did he find out, huh?'

'Same way you find things out for your programme, Gloria. Doing a bit of digging – it's called research.'

She gave a snorting noise, like some animal sneezing.

Arnie went on, smoothly. 'The publicity was bad luck. But everything else worked out okay – as you no doubt know, if you read the story. I was completely cleared. The D.A. didn't even offer any evidence. And the police officer who brought the case is probably gonna be doing traffic duty down in Watts for the next few years.'

'Yeah, trust you to crow at the tragedy of a public servant – a decent police officer doing his duty!'

'I resent that, Miss Gonzales. I resent it very much indeed. You know the facts. And you're distorting them to your own advantage.'

'Listen, you goddam two-bit *pina de huta*! I made it an absolute condition of continuing to retain your services, that there's no more publicity! Whattsa matter with you? You suddenly donna understand Engleesh?' The Hispanic was now coming fast and nasty, although it was hard to tell whether it were meant sarcastically or was genuine.

Becker nodded. 'I think I understand English pretty well, Miss Gonzales. You want me to get you a divorce from your husband? That it?'

'Well sure. But I need grounds – *razones*. Have you found *razones*?'

Becker levelled her with his meanest look. He was beginning to enjoy himself. She was priming herself like a grenade, and when the right moment came, he was going to lean over and pull the pin. 'I've been very busy for the last few days.'

'Yeah, busy trying to beat a drugs rap!'

Arnie felt the first kindling of real anger. 'I would

remind you that I left the court yesterday afternoon without, as the Brits say, a stain on my character.'

'Sure, sure!' Her very white teeth were bared between her shiny scarlet lips; then she leant forward and switched off the recording machine, sat back and gave Arnie a smile that had about as much warmth and charm as a split fingernail. 'Ever heard of no smoke without fire?'

Arnie sat absolutely still for perhaps half a minute. No wonder she'd turned off the recorder. She had virtually stated that he had been guilty all along; and even if she didn't repeat the slander to others, a woman like her could still make a load of trouble for him, if she put her mind to it.

'Miss Gonzales,' he said at last. 'Do I assume that you still want a divorce?'

'Damn right I do! But in my position I can't afford to be anything else but the injured party.'

'Why should you be anything else?' Arnie asked silkily.

'I want to make all the running. I want Mort to be in the wrong. What have you got on him?'

'Your husband – Morton Smellie?'

'Well who else, for Chrissake?' Her anger now seemed tempered by a degree of anxiety. 'I cannot afford scandal, Mr Becker. I cannot afford what they call the "Sleaze Factor". That could ruin me. You understand that?'

'Absolutely, Miss Gonzales.'

'So I gotta be the injured party. *Entendo*?'

'Sure. Though it hardly matters nowadays. These things go through pretty well on the nod.'

'Yeah, but with a fifty-fifty split on all joint assets. Anyway, a divorce for someone like me don't go through no nod! Oh no! It goes through with one helluva lot of noise! That's why I want the details squeaky-clean. I want my viewers to say, There, *la poberita*, she's like the rest of us – she's mortal, she's human, she gets life's brick-bats thrown at her like the rest of us!'

Arnie, who had just been wondering quite the opposite – whether she were really mortal or human – now had a tricky decision to make. If she'd come simply to tell him he was fired, he'd gladly go along with it, except for the outstanding bill from Sherwoods, the P.I. firm. The money would be chicken feed to her – but certainly not to Brackman who'd recently started an economy blitz on light bulbs and paperclips.

But more to the point, if Gloria Gonzales were presented with the Sherwood invoice, she would quite certainly demand to see the results.

On the other hand, taking her chauffeur and limo to the Polo Lounge, the anvil of L.A. gossip, just in order to tell a humble divorce lawyer who'd only met her twice that he was off her case, struck him as slightly baroque, even by L.A. standards. Apart from cutting into her work schedule, even to be seen with Arnie Becker, especially after yesterday's publicity, was surely to risk all kinds of rumour and gossip, in a city that had turned scandal into an art form.

Arnie knew he could afford to wait. He looked at Gloria Gonzales and said nothing. She wasn't used to this. She liked her customers, her picked audience, to respond, to play ball; and Arnie Becker was not playing ball.

'You're not saying a lot, Mr Becker.'

'What would you like me to say?'

'I'd like you to say you're goddam *sorry* you got your name coupled with mine in the paper today.'

He didn't reply.

'And I wanna you say you gotta the real dirt on Mort Smellie, who is a mean little individual who exploits me and runs after anything that wears a skirt.'

'He sounds like Humphrey Bogart,' Arnie said.

She suddenly put her head back and gave a great shout of laughter. 'That I find funny! Oh *Dios*, that is real funny! If you just meet Mort . . .' She paused. '*Have* you seen him?'

'No.'

'Have you got anything on him?'

'Like what?'

She frowned. 'Other women. Booze. Drugs. Y'know.'

'I don't know.' Becker sat still, watching her. And again he wondered at her chameleon-like alternation of mood and speech. Then it clicked. The fierce black eyes, the temper, the undertow of hysteria – it all pointed one way. This paragon of Californian virtue was flying high on cocaine, or some concoction thereof. Bringing him here to the Polo Lounge was just an extra means of getting her kicks in public. She wasn't just an exhibitionist – she was as crazy as a rattlesnake in a beehive.

'I hired you to get all the dirt on my husband Mort. So where is it?'

'Suppose there *isn't* any dirt?'

'Don't be silly. In this city there's dirt on everyone. And if you can't find it, just make it up.'

Arnie nodded at the recording machine on the table between them. 'Just as well that thing's switched off. For you and me.'

'You worried?'

'Not yet, I'm not. But I don't cook up evidence for my clients.'

'Half a million dollars says you do.'

Arnie Becker missed a beat; he swallowed, moistened his lips, tried to swallow again. The Polo Lounge, which was filling up fast now, seemed suddenly dead quiet. To give himself something to do, as well as think, he got out his packet of Abdullah No. 5's and took his time lighting one, but without offering any to Gloria Gonzales who he knew, from her programme, was fiercely anti-smoking.

'Half a million, you said?' He dawdled over the words. 'To do what?'

'Get something that'll stand up in court.'

'Like his pecker?' said Arnie; and she shrieked with laughter.

'You're cute, y'know that?'

'So people are always telling me.' He blew smoke at the ceiling.

She said, 'Is that something interesting you're smoking? It smells real exotic.'

He grinned. 'Just a whiff of one of these, and you'll be swinging blindfold from the chandeliers!'

'Do we have a deal?' Her eyes glistened like black oil.

He drew deep on his cigarette – just like they used to in the movies when he was a boy – and said, still meaning to humour her – no more, 'What about terms of payment? Certified cheque, banker's draft, bearer-bonds, or in a suitcase?'

'You name it, baby!'

Arnie took another drag on his Abdullah No. 5; then, fatally, he laughed. 'What a crazy day!'

She laughed with him – that wild manic laugh that she never let out on TV. 'You're on the team, Arnie.' He smiled, then leant down and brought out his Samsonite case, laying it flat on the table between them.

*

Emily Stallwood gave a loud laugh that showed all her teeth. She leant across the table towards Stuart. 'My husband Marcus is the sort of guy who can charm the monkeys off the trees and he makes such a good impression on people, you'd trust him like a brother. But he's a snake' – she pronounced the words slowly, as though afraid of losing one – 'he is an *asshole*. A-s-s-h-o . . .' Here she gave up and returned to her drink.

The caviar arrived and she immediately complained, 'Such tiny portions!' – and Stuart at once doubled the order.

He returned to the matter of Marcus Stallwood. 'Emily, is your husband tied up with any rackets?'

She took some time answering. She finished her first helping of caviar and started on the second dollop as soon as it was spooned out by the waiter. When she spoke it was with her mouth full. 'D'ya mean is he squeaky-clean? Hell, I guess not. Who is in California – except the bums and the old hippies, I guess.'

'Emily, I have to know this, if I'm to help you get

some of his money. Is he involved with the Mob?'

'*Whaaaat!*' Her mouth fell open like a mailbox. 'My husband in the Mob? *The Mafia!* Are you outta your tiny mind, Stuart?' Her voice was thickening now, but whether by accident or design he couldn't decide.

'You see, Emily, the fact of the matter is, if I'm to help you – both as a lawyer and as a friend – I've got to know what we're up against.'

'*We?*'

'Well, I'll be involved if you start divorce proceedings.'

'Well, I told you, only way I get to cut free from that Marcus is by getting a big slice of the loot.'

'You're not answering my question, Emily.'

'Huh?'

'Is – or was, at any time – your husband involved in the rackets? The Syndicates? The Mob?'

'Jeez, Mr Markowitz, you really gonna get us both in a lotta trouble! You get your balls cut off with talk like that! My, he once had a guy bounce a cheque on" him – just a couple of hundred bucks, it was – and he had all the guy's fingers broken on his right hand. The hand that wrote the cheque, see. Only the funny thing was, the guy was left-handed!' She seemed to think this so funny that she started to choke on the chopped onion that came with the caviar.

He banged her several times on the back and made her drink some water, and when she recovered she was still laughing, tears in her eyes. 'You must admit that's funny, huh, Stuart?'

He suddenly didn't have any appetite anymore. He didn't even want the champagne. My God, he thought, was everyone at McKenzie Brackman just innocent babes in the wood? Arnie Becker going to a surprise party on the beach and not noticing there were drugs. And Stuart Markowitz, the firm's tax wizard, wining and dining the wife of a mobster, all in the quest of separating the man from his ill-gotten gains. It was crazy. And he was a fool. He had already lost his wife. Now he was threatened with something even worse. For just the idea of physical violence made him feel sick and giddy.

The waiter arrived with the main course, but Emily Stallwood turned up her nose at it. 'Ugh, those birds, they're so messy to eat! Let's have some more caviar!' The waiter looked deferentially at Stuart. He just managed to smile. 'Bring one more portion of caviar, please.'

'Very good, sir.'

Until then, Emily Stallwood had been slurring her words, and her thoughts seemed poorly co-ordinated; but from now on she started to get properly drunk. She finished the bottle of Krug and made Stuart order another. He tried to talk to her about her husband's finances, to keep the conversation on a business-like level, but it was like trying to keep a child amused.

Several times – such as when he tried explaining about the possibility of serving a garnishee order on a bank account in London – she interrupted by making a crudely erotic suggestion that made him blench. *Oh God, what have I let myself in for?* he thought.

Instinct told him to get up and walk out. Give his address to the head waiter. They must be used to having people walk out on their guests before now. He could feel he was sweating. He touched his forehead and it felt cold and slimy. His collar was too tight. He swallowed and his mouth was dry. He drank some champagne but it had a rough, acid taste, and gave him no pleasure.

Emily Stallwood was saying, with a slow, sodden emphasis, 'What I wanna do, you an' me, Stuart, is we bust into my bastard husband's banks all over and we take off, like we go to Mexico, like Acapulco, and we check in somewhere really fancy and we have a great, big, big, enormous bed and we just *eat each other*! Whatdya say, *mon petit*? That means 'my little one'. Ya don' mind we calling you that, d'ya, because that's what y'are, my lill' Stuart – my lill' baby-lawyer friend who's gonna get me real serious rich . . . !'

Her words reached him from further and further away, like the sound of pebbles being dropped down an ever-deepening well. A mist formed in front of his eyes, so that he had the strange experience of seeing everything in black and white. It was like an old movie, but now even the sound was fading.

He heard her repeating, '*real seriously rich!*' and suddenly he couldn't understand what she meant. There was a pain in his arm and he felt he couldn't breathe. He started to stand up; a waiter appeared, and he fell gently, totally into the waiter's arms, and the film stopped.

20

Arnie Opens The Case

It was a few minutes before one o'clock. All around was the soft roar of the rich and famous indulging in social intercourse.

With a smooth, decisive gesture Arnie Becker snapped open the Samsonite case and slid it across the table, where Gloria Gonzales could examine its contents at leisure.

To an untrained eye there was nothing obviously salacious or sensational in any of the photographs inside the case. Most had been taken outdoors, probably with a zoom lens from inside a parked car. They mainly showed Gloria Gonzales in various smart, glittering outfits, going into and coming out of two different buildings, which were evidently luxury apartments or condominiums. And every time she was on the arm of a well-built man with blond hair and the kind of classic good looks that went out with Errol Flynn.

However, some photographs showed the inside of a luxurious car with various limbs entwined together. A bottle of champagne in a cooler was stashed in one corner, a plate of oyster shells on one of the tray-tables.

Three different cars featured in the pictures: a Fleetwood, a Porsche and a Mercedes; and there were separate zoom lens pics of the numberplates: two were L.A.; one – on the Fleetwood – was Las Vegas.

The nearest any of the photos came to being 'hot' or suggestive was a set of night shots, taken with an infra-red camera outside what looked like a restaurant or out-of-town night spot, showing them both in fuzzy orange profile, kissing passionately. In several the man was squeezing her buttocks with both hands and her skirt was riding up her thighs.

The pictures came with a computerised print-out from Sherwoods. Times, dates, locations. All the cars were registered in the name of Marcus Bolder Stallwood, aged 47, married, with no children. There were two addresses, both in his name, but neither were the family home. His profession was described simply as 'corporate financier'.

His name meant nothing to Arnie. The addresses and the three cars certainly indicated a degree of wealth; but certainly not one of the rich and famous who litter the society pages and gossip mags. Just a well-to-do adulterer taking a bit of time off to screw one of the famous women in America. Who was it who said that fame is the greatest aphrodisiac?

Arnie noticed a strange quiet that seemed to have descended on their table in the corner. It was like the silence from inside a telephone booth. And with it, a terrible, charged intimacy.

Gloria Gonzales' face had imperceptibly, but totally, changed. Arnie found himself looking at a grim Aztec mask. Her slightly flared nostrils, suggesting Indian blood, were pinched white; her eyes were dead black buttons; her mouth a fleshy bloodless aperture that dispensed nothing but pure, distilled hatred.

He had expected her to scream, to fly at his throat, to throw the kind of tantrum that would boost her next show by a million or so. But there was none of that. She wasn't aggressive. A casual passer-by would have said she seemed almost bored.

She looked at the photographs once, then flicked back through them, methodically, as she would with publicity stills. Finally she said, in a flat neutral voice,

'You are offering to sell me these, are you, Mr Becker?'

He sounded genuinely offended. 'What on earth do you take me for, Miss Gonzales?'

'I take you for what you are. A blackmailer.'

Becker started to protest, but she held up her hand. 'Please, spare me your horrible humility. Just tell me how you got these pictures?'

He told her – truthfully, as it happened – how the P.I. had been put on the wrong person, when the surveillance had been meant, of course, for her husband. He added that his main purpose in coming to meet her here was to explain the mix-up and make clear, as politely as he could, that he did not want any further involvement in her personal affairs.

He could not tell from her face or demeanour whether she were convinced or not. For at this point she stood up and asked him to excuse her. She was going to what she coyly described as 'the little girls' room'.

Arnie's chosen profession, as a divorce lawyer in L.A., had made him inured to all manner of reactions, when people had their private lives exposed to outside scrutiny. He'd found Gloria Gonzales a good deal more controlled than most – but as an experienced TV performer that was perhaps not so surprising. On the other hand, that same star status meant that she certainly had more to lose than most.

She had been gone just over ten minutes now. Arnie had glanced round to look for her two minders, but there was no sign of them. On the table in front of him was his empty glass of Campari and the Samsonite attaché case which was now closed but unlocked. To give himself something to do, he opened it – after making sure that no-one could see – and began looking through the pictures again.

When he next looked at his watch, it was coming up to a quarter past one. She'd been gone nearly twenty minutes. He stood up and looked out for her, thinking she might be chatting to someone at the bar. There was no sign of her; nor of the two crew-cut minders.

He waited another ten minutes, then called for the check, paid with his Amex Gold Card, and picked up his attaché case, after making sure it was locked, then strolled out to the front of the lounge. Jane Fonda had gone, but there were now at least half a dozen familiar faces from film and TV. A fat man in a hideous seersucker suit was yelling, 'I wasn't saying it was the worst movie he ever made! I said if Woody Allen had made it . . . !'

Arnie stopped a waiter. 'You see where Gloria Gonzales went?'

He frowned. 'Who are you, sir?'

'I've been having a drink with her. She went out to the ladies' room about a quarter of an hour ago.'

'You'd better ask at the door. I haven't seen her.'

Arnie went out to the desk where they took reservations, as well as discreetly screening out the chaff from the wheat.

'Yeah, she left about ten minutes ago.'

'Alone?'

'I guess so. I didn't see anyone. Except the chauffeur, of course.'

'You sure it was her?' Arnie asked, rather desperately.

210

'You think I'd miss a face like that? Anyway, what is it to you?'

'I was having a drink with her.'

'Oh yeah?' He began to look curious. 'You mean she stood you up?'

'Not exactly. Sort of business talk . . .' He thought the man was showing too much interest, so he moved away. If she'd left alone, perhaps the two minders were still here. But why? She'd hardly want to get tough in a place like the Polo Lounge? It would be like carrying out a bank robbery on prime-time TV.

He checked round the lobby and the other bar in the hotel, in case she'd found someone to talk to there. She'd certainly think nothing of keeping a mere lawyer waiting.

But there was no sign of her, and no sign of her muscle-men.

He went back to the man at the desk, gave him a five dollar bill and asked him to get him a cab. He gave a short gesture to another flunkey outside who whistled and a white Chrysler appeared. Arnie went out and gave the second man another five dollar bill. Jeez, I'm in the wrong job! he thought, as he got in and gave the driver the address of the office.

He sat back, cradling the attaché case with both arms, and tried to work out what conclusions to draw.

*

As soon as Abby had taken the call from the 12th Precinct house in downtown Inglewood, she rushed breathlessly into Michael Kuzak's office.

211

'Oh Mike, it's him again! I can't bear it!'

Kuzak removed his feet from the desk, on which were piled the stacks of tax documents, each representing one of the case-loads on which Stuart Markowitz had been working, just prior to being rushed into hospital. Kuzak decided that if he'd been Stuart, he'd have considered himself lucky. Every page of each document, with their yards of small print and enormous figures, made about as much compelling reading to Kuzak as an annual Supervisors' Report on Rodent Control for Greater L.A., with relevant appendices attached.

She stood wide-eyed in the doorway. 'Are you very busy?'

'D'you mean, do I want to break off and hold your hand?'

'Oh Mike, it's the Count. He's being held at the 12th Precinct in Inglewood.'

'How did he get down there? I thought the *Pacific Review* offices were up on Wilshire?'

'Yeah they are. Only this has got nothing to do with the *Pacific Review*. He'd gone down to see his co-author, Randell Shaw. Remember? They were collaborating on a film script for one of the big studios and they had a fight.'

'A fight over a verb, wasn't it?'

'Yep. They were both suing each other for assault.'

'And now?'

'I don't know exactly. But it seems they got together again and started to work, and then they had another argument. Police were called, and now they're both in the slammer.'

212

'And you want me to come along with you and bail him out?' Kuzak stood up. 'Get Roxanne call us a cab – one that's prepared to go into Inglewood and wait. It's not the kind of neighbourhood you park a car in, and not exactly a place where you pick up a cruising cab.'

Kuzak made a couple of calls, to tell clients that Stuart Markowitz was unwell, but would be returning soon to the office. Then he rode down in the elevator with Abby and they both got in the cab that was waiting outside.

The driver half turned his head and said, 'I told the lady that I charge double to go to Inglewood, and I charge three times to wait. I keep all the windows locked. Okay?' He wore a baseball cap, had a bull-neck and spoke with a thick German accent.

'Maybe we should have hired an armoured personnel carrier?' Kuzak said.

'Yeah.' Before he pulled away, the driver opened the glove compartment, groped deep inside and came out with a well-oiled pistol. He weighed it in his hand. 'Walther PPK. Beautiful, huh?'

'Great,' said Kuzak. 'Even better than the movies.'

*

The 12th Precinct House looked like the command post in some Third World city at war. There were irregular gaps of wasteland between brick tenements, some of which were burnt out, others boarded up. The side-walks were humped and cracked, as by a minor earth-quake; and near the Precinct house were three wrecks

213

of cars, all gutted and without wheels, and one charred black.

'This is the sort of scene that makes me want to vote communist,' Kuzak said under his breath, as they got out. The place seemed deserted, except for a group of tall teenagers wheeling and dodging about on roller-skates.

The desk sergeant had a big round head like a stone, with about as much expression. Kuzak said briskly, 'I'm a lawyer and I'm here to represent Count Oblomov.'

The man thought about this for a few seconds, looked at Abby, then back to Kuzak and said, 'Sign,' as he slid a big dog-eared ledger across the desk. 'And the lady?' he added.

'We're both representing him,' said Kuzak, pushing the ledger back. 'What are the charges exactly?'

'Drunk. Fighting. Causing a disturbance in a public place.'

'You got them both down there?'

'Yeah.'

'And the other man – is he called Shaw?'

'Yeah. Says he's in the movies.'

'Has he called a lawyer?'

'Nope. Still sleeping it off.'

'The other guy – Oblomov – what's the bail?'

'To get him outta here?' The sergeant gave a malignant grin. 'For a C you can have him. Me, I wouldn't give a used bus ticket for either of them.'

'I'd like to see him first.' Kuzak turned to Abby. 'You'd better stay – unless you want to see the monkey-house.'

She said, 'I'll stay here.'

The sergeant pinged a bell and a colossus of a man, a black who made Mike Tyson look puny, bent almost double to get through the door and stood holding a ring of keys. 'Show this gentleman down to the Count's suite, Jacko.'

Jacko shot a quick, appraising look at Abby, then led Kuzak out and down a cement stairway that smelt faintly of vomit and disinfectant. The row of cells were a lot quieter than Kuzak expected. About half were occupied. In one a middle-aged man was crying. There was another lying on his back, singing snatches of *South Pacific*.

Count Oblomov was sitting on the floor with his thin legs drawn up under his chin, and with his eyes closed. He was no longer wearing the head bandage, and between his long thinning grey hair was a thick welt of black blood; but to his previous wounds were now added fresh injuries. His thin aristocratic nose was swollen up like an aubergine, and both eyes were a dark livid blue and yellow, while his upper lip, split open for the second time in as many days, was raw and bloody, like some leftover in a butcher's shop.

'Hey you!' the sergeant growled, and unlocked the barred door. 'Your lawyer's here!'

The Russian looked up, focusing with difficulty. Kuzak walked in. 'Count Oblomov?'

'Yes. I don't know you.'

Kuzak caught a whiff of the man's breath: it was as though a tomb had just been opened. 'My name's Michael Kuzak and I'm going bail for you for a hundred bucks.'

'But that girl – the pretty one . . . ?'

'She's upstairs. I was just sparing your feelings. Let's go.'

The Russian shambled with him to the door, then glanced down the row of cells. 'Where is that bastard Shaw?' he said venomously.

'He's asleep,' said Jacko. 'And I don't want him woken.'

The three of them went upstairs. Abby kept her distance when she saw the Count. Kuzak signed the bail papers, handed over one of the firm's cheques, and they went outside.

In the taxi Kuzak, who was sitting in the middle, said, 'Just tell me what happened?'

The Count said that a man from the studio had come round that morning and given him a thousand dollars to get on with the script. He was driven down to where Shaw lived – 'in a really horrible little house because his third wife has nearly bankrupted him and taken his great Hollywood palace away' – and the man from the studio had given Shaw a thousand dollars and told them both to get on with the work.

'When's the deadline?' said Kuzak.

'Oh that's a long time ago.'

'So when do they want it now?'

'The end of the week. Then we each get five thousand dollars.'

'Well you're not gonna get it at this rate. So how did the cops get in on the act?'

'Ah, we had some lunch and went to a bar, you know, to wet the whistle.'

'Yeah – and?'

'Shaw he got disgustingly drunk. He was drunk when I arrived. I think he is perhaps an alcoholic.'

'So you *both* got drunk?'

'I cannot create when I am sober,' the Russian said, shrugging his shoulders, as though it were an elementary fact.

'So who started the fight?' said Kuzak, opening his window several inches. The Russian's breath was getting on his nerves.

'Well it was like this – we had a very long, bad argument about Czar Nicholas the Second and about Kerensky . . .'

Kuzak said, for Abby's benefit, 'Kerensky was the last Russian prime-minister, before the Communists took over in 1917.' He turned back to the Count. 'So what then happened between you and Shaw?'

'Shaw is a fool – he is one of the old Hollywood lefties. He understands nothing about Russia. He is a drunken Hollywood hack – what is called a Bollinger Bolshevik!'

'Quite,' said Kuzak. 'But what was the *substance* of the argument?'

'He insulted Czar Nicholas.'

'Is that all?'

'*All!*' The Russian roared.

Kuzak felt Abby cringe at his side, and saw the driver watching Count Oblomov carefully in his mirror. 'Nicholas was a holy man! He was a saint! The Little Father of all Russians. Then what did we get? We got that vulgar little bastard Lenin – sent to us by the Devil! And since then we have been bleeding to death! All because of people like Shaw who thinks that the sun still shines out of Karl Marx's ass!'

'Sounds a little behind the times,' murmured Kuzak. 'And so you hit him?'

'Not immediately. It was when he said that if it weren't for Stalin, Hitler would have ruled the world.'

Kuzak refrained from commenting on this.

'That is when I hit him,' the Russian said, as though it were a perfectly natural sequence of events.

'And that was it? The barman called the cops?'

Count Oblomov nodded. 'It was a matter of honour. Where are we going now?'

'Back to the office. We'll clean you up a bit, then take you home.'

The Russian nodded again; and it occurred to Kuzak that in the man's distorted social spectrum, being his hired lawyer counted for about as much as a footman or valet. Certainly he offered neither Kuzak nor Abby a word of thanks.

21

Whispers in the
Steam Room

Leland McKenzie was feeling better than he'd done since coming into hospital. He was beginning to fret and complain. He'd even had his personal computer and word processor brought round by the 'Valley Girls', Candice and Jayne, who spent nearly an hour fussing over Leland, puffing up his pillows and making sure the air-conditioning was absolutely right.

He had also bullied the hospital administration to install a second telephone line. At first the staff had been indulgent, but they were now becoming a little anxious. The staff nurse told him he'd been very seriously ill and that a heavy workload was the very worst thing he could contemplate.

But Leland would have none of it. He was full of anecdotes about colleagues who'd fallen dead in the gym or on the golf-course, and one man younger than him who'd taken early retirement and dropped dead out of sheer boredom.

It was in this mood, of upbeat grumpiness, that Douglas Brackman found him, sitting up in bed with both phones active, his bare chest and upper arms still sprouting tubes and wires that were connected to what looked like a large computer.

'Hang on. I'll be right back to you. Douglas – take a chair. Yep. Yep. Well, of course! You think I'd turn down an invitation like that? It's like being invited to dinner with Lucille Ball! What . . . ? Yes, well I know she's dead.

'Just sit down, Douglas. I think I'd better call you straight back. No, this is business. I *can't* put you on hold – I'm in hospital . . .'

Brackman sat and watched this performance with a

look of grim amusement. He waited until both phones were idle, then said, 'I'd think it tragic, if I didn't know that most of those guys you call will probably be dead before you are.'

'That's handsome of you, Douglas! No, I don't think I've ever felt better.'

'Is it the nurses or the drugs?'

'That's slander, Douglas. Just put it down to room service.' He smiled contentedly. 'No doubt you come as the bearer of bad news? What fresh calamity has just struck the good ship, McKenzie Brackman?'

'Nothing solid, Leland. It's just that with you being sick, and all the other upsets at the office, I guess I've been getting paranoid.'

'C'mon, Douglas, better out than in! What's eating you?'

'It's about that thing Igor Strauss told you.'

'So?' Leland McKenzie's face darkened. 'What about it?'

'Well, yesterday I heard something else on the same lines. What I'd call an inspired rumour.'

'Inspired by whom?'

Brackman paid a mental tribute to Leland McKenzie's immaculate grammar. 'Well, I was at the Athletic Club last night and I got talking to a guy who'd been in the steam room and said he'd heard a couple of guys schmoozing who mentioned the name McKenzie Brackman . . .'

'In what connection?'

'They were talking about that New York firm, Radcliffe, Noach and Williams, which is opening a branch office in L.A. You know Igor told you he reckoned they were head-hunting two of our people? Apparently, they're looking for reliable employees who can keep secrets. I guess that rules out about half the population of L.A.'

He paused, as a willowy black nurse came in and started to take Leland's blood pressure. 'You're not getting all agitated and over-excited, are you, Mr Leland?'

He gave her a bleak grin. 'This is my partner. He's trying to kill me, so he can take over the business.'

She laughed, then stood looking at her watch, timing his heartbeats. 'It's a little high, Mr McKenzie. You really gotta rest while you're here.'

Leland waved a hand to her. 'I didn't invite him. He comes every day. And every day he tells me some fresh calamity.'

'You gotta get better, and that means rest and no worries,' she said, utterly detached and indifferent to the troubles and intrigues of McKenzie Brackman. She was in the business of life and death.

McKenzie waited until she'd left, then said, 'So the firm was mentioned in the steam room? But you didn't hear it yourself?'

'No. Just hearsay evidence. This firm from New York are just all around L.A., trying to skim off the cream. And because McKenzie Brackman have been keeping a pretty high profile lately, mediawise . . .'

Leland McKenzie groaned. 'Don't use those appalling words, Douglas – leave them to the advertising agencies and the Pentagon. *Mediawise*, my sainted mother!' There was a pause. Leland enjoyed these moments of *gravitas*, at the expense of his junior part-

223

ner. 'So. Did your steam room source indicate whose head, or heads, were being hunted?'

Brackman cleared his throat. He found doing business sitting on Leland's bed faintly ridiculous. 'Not even a hint. Except that it's general knowledge that they intend to set up a really big operation here in L.A.'

Leland's eyes narrowed over his bifocals. 'They haven't head-hunted *you*, have they, Douglas?'

Brackman felt himself flush hotly, like a teenager. He had honestly never considered such a possibility. He struggled to convince Leland, and knew that by protesting too much, he was being thoroughly unconvincing. 'But what on earth made you think such a thing?' he said finally.

'Just that when I first told you about Igor Strauss coming in and telling me about two people leaving us, you didn't seem all that worried. That's not like you. You fret about everything.'

'Well, maybe it's the tension, the insecurity – and the overwork. I'm a natural worrier, Leland – you know that. Anyway, I swear it wasn't me.'

'Sure, I just wanted to check. Anyway, you'd be miserable if you didn't have something to worry about. Maybe you should think of having a coronary!'

As he spoke there was a sharp rap on the door, and the black nurse came in, followed by a well-groomed woman in a dark-blue uniform, whom Leland knew as one of the hospital administrators.

'Yes, Mrs Turner, what can I do for you?' Leland asked, with mock solemnity. 'Or rather, what can you do for me?'

'Mr McKenzie, you have in your employ a Mr Stuart Markowitz?'

'What's happened to him?' both McKenzie and Brackman asked in unison.

'He's just down the corridor. I think they've finished with him now. He should be all right.'

'But what's *happened* to him?' they cried.

'He had a slight coronary. Very slight, I'm glad to report. He was in a restaurant and I think he got overcome by the heat.'

'How long will he be here?' asked McKenzie.

'Have you called his wife?' said Brackman.

'His wife's on her way. She seemed very upset, naturally.'

'But how long –?' McKenzie asked again.

'We may keep him in for a couple of days, for observation.'

'Well,' said McKenzie drily. 'If Radcliffe, Noach and Williams are thinking of head-hunting Stuart, I guess they've got another think coming!'

*

Arnie sat back in the cab, watching the rim of the Pacific coming into view, with the palms tossing their heads in a light ocean breeze. Until now the driver, a thick-set man in a black leather jerkin, had not spoken. They had turned on to Lincoln Boulevard, coming into Venice, when he looked at Arnie in the mirror and said, 'You expect company back there?'

'What?' Arnie looked puzzled. 'Company?'

'Porsche. Two cars back. Been tailing us from the hotel.'

'Jesus!' Arnie turned and peered out at the steady three lane procession of traffic. Two cars back – just as the driver said – on the inside lane, was a dark blue Porsche saloon with smoked windows. Sort of automobile you see between Beverly Hills and the Ocean as often as you see a good nose job.

Arnie shrugged. 'Why d'you think they're tailing us?'

The driver also shrugged. 'Let's find out.' He slipped the car from automatic on to manual and, without giving a signal, surged out into the fast lane against a crescendo of hooting, as the speedometer crept up over sixty, seventy . . .

'You pay the fine – okay?' The driver seemed to be enjoying himself.

Arnie had twisted round and was watching the dark blue car as it stayed penned in by the three ranks of cars, drawing back further and further. Suddenly it swerved, cutting like a dagger through the column on the centre lane, then dodging back diagonally on to the hard shoulder, to take advantage of a short gap; before coming out again into the fast lane, right across the bows of half a dozen cars, breaking every rule in the book. It was right behind the taxi now, the driver no doubt guessing he'd been rumbled and not caring now whether Arnie saw them or not.

Arnie started to think fast. To try and take him in a cab in broad daylight was crazy! He'd have the driver as an independent witness, for a start. What did Gloria hope to gain? The photographs? They were only prints.

Or did she think that by having him followed, she could somehow track down the negatives?

Arnie Becker had never thought of himself as a coward; but neither was he particularly brave. His hands now felt damp and there was sweat starting up under his shirt. He wondered, in a distracted moment, how Gloria Gonzales' lunch was going. She'd had a date after their meeting at noon. Or was that just for decor? She wouldn't want anyone to think she'd be alone for lunch. But where had the two well-scrubbed goons gone? Could they be in that car behind? And could the car have been waiting near the hotel entrance, ready for just this contingency?

But that would only make sense if Gloria Gonzales were psychic. And there was another thing; from the moment that he'd shown her the pictures, to the time when he'd left alone in the cab, had been less than half an hour. And the actual time that Gloria had been gone from the table – allegedly in the ladies' *comfort station* – was *little more than twenty minutes*. Hardly time to organise a grand slam kidnapping.

When he next turned to look out of the back, he got a shock. The dark-blue Porsche had gone. The traffic had thinned as they came near the Yacht Club, and he could see the cars behind strung out for perhaps a quarter of a mile. No sign of the Porsche. He told the driver this, and the man shrugged. 'I lost him, huh?'

'I guess so,' Arnie said. He felt oddly cheated.

'Woman trouble, huh? Husband trouble – huh?' He spoke in short little grunts, beating time on the steering wheel. 'All I know, this is a bad town to make enemies in. Guy I knew, drove a cab, got to takin' out a married

227

woman. Husband got to find out, called up the cab station – called up seven times till he got the right one, then blew the guy away, right inside his own cab. Ruined the goddam upholstery – leopard skin he'd done the seats in.' He shook his head. 'Guy's got to be careful in a town like this.'

Then suddenly it clicked for Arnie: like watching the spinning drums of a fruit machine, and seeing all the oranges line up one by one for the jackpot.

He laid the attaché case flat on his knees, unlocked it and opened it carefully so the driver couldn't see the contents. He riffled through a few of the prints, found one he was looking for, then double-checked with the Sherwood print-out. He closed the case and locked it.

How he could be so dumb? Or had he just been too confident, too laid back, content to play games with the bitch-goddess of the Chat Show, and somehow expect her to concede with grace when she lost?

He looked at the back, and again there was no Porsche. Out of sight, out of mind, he thought. Like hell! Something like this didn't just go away. He was wondering how much he could safely tell them at the office. Or how little. Probably nothing for the moment, he thought, as the cab stopped outside the office block.

The meter showed twenty-two dollars. Arnie gave the driver a fifty note.

'You know what?' the man said. 'I been driving a cab in L.A. for nearly twenty years, and I never been in a car chase till today! I feel like I just hit a home run for the Yankees!'

22

A Compulsive Litigant

'Just tell me how *old* you think he is?'

Kuzak shrugged. 'Fifty? Fifty-five?'

'He is seventy-one years old!' Abby cried. 'He should be in a rest home!'

'Or a cage. You worked out yet if he can pay?'

'Oh Mike, that must be the biggest laugh since Bing Crosby and Bob Hope split up. I've been on to Records, the P.D., State licensing authority, and the morgues of both *The L.A. Clarion* and *Los Angeles Times*. First, he ain't no Count. He first came to the States in 1954, after defecting through Vienna. I suspect at first he got fed a few breadcrumbs by the C.I.A.'

'That would figure,' Kuzak growled. 'Trust the Company to pick winners!'

'And his name is not Oblomov. He took that as a pseudonym for his writing, because he claimed the K.G.B. might have taken out a contract on him.'

'One time we need them, the K.G.B. isn't there!'

'His real name's Grodek. Anton Grodek, registered as a freelance writer and translator. God knows what he lives on. He's got no money. He has two separate bank loans clocking up interest. And the I.R.S. would like to talk to him.'

'And he's your client, honey.'

'He's *our* client, Michael.'

They were talking in Kuzak's office where he'd been labouring through Stuart Markowitz's latest case, before he was struck down. 'Is our *Mister* Oblomov a full U.S. citizen?' he asked finally.

'Yes. That's the only thing he's got going for him. He's also a professional litigant. We're the seventh law firm he's been to. The others won't touch him again.

He's sued three of them – one successfully. He's sued NBC for misrepresentation and lost. He's sued two publishers – one here in L.A., the other in New York – and both settled before going to court.'

Kuzak groaned. 'Tell me something to cheer me up, Abby.'

She grinned. 'Sure. Earlier this year he sued City Hall for ruining his suit.'

'*What!*'

'He'd just been sent a very expensive suit from a mail order firm in London. Harris tweed, according to the court transcript. He bought it, he said, out of royalties from a book called *The Practical Jokes of J. V. Stalin.*

'And the first thing he did after putting on the suit was go up to Griffith Park and sit on a bench that had just been repainted a bright green. He said that when he stood up he looked like an expletive deleted zebra.

'The defence tried to claim that the suit was a fifty dollar job, made in Taiwan. They also claimed the Parks Authority had clearly marked the bench with a Wet Paint sign. But the jury found for Oblomov, and he got a thousand dollars.'

'All on the contingency basis?' said Kuzak.

'Oh *natch*!' Abby said tartly, folding her arms.

'And with us too?'

''Fraid so. Forty percent if we win, zero if we lose.'

'He was your client, Abby. Why didn't you check him out on that first day?'

'Because I didn't have time. Leland put him on to me and he took him on as a favour to a friend. I was counting on him to help me out. Anyway, you don't expect a member of the Soviet aristocracy to have a record.'

She hesitated, then said softly, 'Leland. Just before he got ill.' She had flushed down to her neckline, ashamed of her petty act of betrayal in blaming Leland's good intentions. 'Don't tell anyone, will you, Mike?'

'Wouldn't do any good if I did. Anyway, he's facing at least three criminal charges – assault, destruction of property and drunk and disorderly. There won't be any contingency on that lot! And if the *Pacific Review* decides to go after him for repairs to their office, we're not even looking at Zero – more like a Black Hole.'

'Could he go to jail? I'd hate that.'

'Oh I don't know – jail might suit his dark Slavonic soul rather well. But I guess if we plead his age, and suggest some degree of diminished responsibility, we might get him a "suspended". He might even become a minor celebrity with all those Republicans who don't like the *Pacific Review*.'

She stood up and started towards the door. 'By the way, seen anything of Grace lately?'

'No. Why?'

'No reason. 'Bye.'

Kuzak sat for several minutes twirling a pencil between his fingers and staring at Markowitz's files.

*

The studio was dark. Furniture lay stacked against the walls or grouped pointlessly in small islands. Clusters of lights stood among the props. The only sound was the soft clatter of a computer keyboard, the greenish light of the screen illuminating a small area.

At the far end of the studio, a door was pushed cautiously open. The tap of high heels. A swish of taffeta. Expensive scent. The man at the keyboard rose to his feet and crossed the floor.

In the darkness they clasped each other passionately. 'We'll have to stop seeing each other for a while,' she said. 'Things are getting tough. We've been found out.'

He held her tight, catching his breath. 'Found out?'

'There was someone following me, like I thought. That fool of a lawyer – I should never have gone to him. He set a P.I. on *me* instead of Mort!'

Reassured that his darker secrets had not been discovered, he murmured, 'We'll make this time really special. Let's go to the design department. It's not ideal, but at least there's a door that locks.' In fact, he was quite relieved. With all his other commitments, he was growing tired of this particular subterfuge.

Together, they hurried across the studio carefully avoiding the cables waiting to trap them. Once in the room, he turned the key and then embraced her again. Gently, he pushed her towards one of the tables. 'I guess this is the origin of the expression "back to the drawing board" . . .'

Her taffeta dress rustled loudly in the silence.

23

Roxanne to the
Rescue

It was pure coincidence that Leland McKenzie and Stuart Markowitz left hospital at the same time; though, perhaps on the principle of 'first in, last out', Leland left an hour after Stuart.

The task of transporting them, and their considerable luggage – particularly Leland's – required some logistical planning; and since the firm was already two short, most of the spadework was left to the 'Valley Girls', Candice and Jayne.

However, both seemed curiously subdued when they arrived; and while Leland was being wheeled along to the elevator, he thought both girls were going to break down and cry. At the last moment, Ann Kelsey arrived to take care of Stuart. Since he'd been admitted, she'd made a point of visiting him at least twice a day, but only for short periods on account of her own workload.

Douglas Brackman was in court, pleading for the disappointed actor who'd bombarded the studio chief, whom he claimed had cheated them, with mail-order dresses and copies of *American Psycho*. Douglas was hoping to get the guy to plead guilty and apologise, so he could go back and take charge of the office. In the end, the actor was sentenced to a hundred hours' community work, but this was more than compensated by his already having been offered a part in a big budget movie, produced by one of his victim's rivals.

Arnie Becker was lounging about the office, with a somewhat preoccupied air. He was still officially on Gloria Gonzales' divorce case; but after the bizarre events of yesterday, he not only felt undecided, but downright scared.

He wondered what the hell had made him show his

hand so blatantly in public. It was like a poker player showing the table his first three cards. No – worse. His whole hand. Sure, he'd shown similar photographs to women in public places before, but that was because he felt they'd be less likely to get hysterical in a restuarant or bar than in his office.

He tried to rationalise what he'd done. He had not liked Gloria Gonzales from the moment they met. Even *before* he'd met her. He found her show, the few times he'd seen it, repulsive; he hated that hyped self-righteousness, the coy aggressiveness, the implied assertion that she was the Tribune of the American People.

And he now forced himself to admit that not only had he wanted to turn the tables on her – after she'd thrown the tantrum about the publicity in the papers – but secretly he'd also wanted to master her, even scare her. Teach her that no-one – not even Gloria Gonzales – could tangle with ace-lawyer Arnie Becker and walk away untouched.

He was nervous. He even broke the house rules and smoked a few cigarettes between cups of black coffee. He badly wanted someone in whom he could confide: to seek the advice of someone who knew the rules and how to play this sort of game. *Goddammit! He needed a lawyer!* Trouble was, the moment he told anyone, the thing became semi-official: and he was all too aware that his conduct over the past two days was not exemplary.

The office seemed strangely deserted. McKenzie and Markowitz were being chauffeured back to their respective homes. Ann Kelsey had taken the day off to get her husband settled in. Abby had volunteered to do the same for Leland McKenzie. Brackman was still in court. And Sifuentes had been called out by the American Council for Civil Liberies to plead for a Nicaraguan who'd been in the country seven years and had now been declared an illegal immigrant.

Even the 'Valley Girls' seemed to have taken the day off. Normally, Arnie found their chattering and giggling around the office highly irritating; but now that they weren't here he realised he almost missed them. No-one to fetch him coffee, or to let him catch a quick glimpse up their skirts, which they frequently did.

Now, at just after four o'clock in the afternoon, Arnie Becker was alone in the office except for Roxanne and Michael Kuzak.

He smoked a couple more cigarettes, then wandered along to Kuzak's office. 'Hi, Mike.'

'Hi, Arnie.'

'Anything interesting?'

Kuzak shrugged and snapped his fingernail across one of half a dozen files on his desk. 'Just doing a bit of tidying for Stuart and his ladyfriend.'

'The one Ann Kelsey threw him outta the house over? You never believed that story, did you? Not our little Stuart!'

'Well, y'know what they say? It's always the quiet ones.' Kuzak sat up and adjusted his shirt sleeves. 'Although if Stuart is still thinking of playing hookie, I'd strongly counsel him to keep well away from this lady.'

'Yeah? Something nasty in the woodshed?'

'It'd have to be a damn big woodshed!' Kuzak sat

forward, drumming his fingers on the files. 'If Stuart –
or anyone else – handed this stuff into the D.A.'s
Office, the lady-in-question's husband would find himself looking at ten to thirty – and that's even before the
Revenue boys get their claws into him.'

'So is it your responsibility? Or Stuart's?'

'It's a good point, Arnie. I've been thinking about it
most of the afternoon. In fact, I've been thinking
maybe one of us might just let these files go missing.
Most of them are Stuart's original research, anyway, so
nobody'd notice.'

'But the wife hired Stuart?'

'Yep. She's hoping he might find a loophole so she
can get her hands on some of her husband's loot after
she's divorced him.'

'Does she know?'

'Know what?'

'That her husband's a crook?'

Kuzak shrugged. 'I guess you'd better ask Stuart. But
if he doesn't watch his step here, he's gonna be thinking
a coronary is the least of his problems. I'd say Mrs
Emily Stallwood is a very dangerous –'

'*What did you say?*' Arnie had leapt out of his chair as
though he'd just found he was sitting on a rattlesnake.

Kuzak stared at him.

'That name?' Arnie yelled, 'Mrs –?'

'Emily Stallwood. Why?'

'*Jesus!* Come to my office – I got something to show
you.'

The Samsonite case was locked in Arnie's wall safe.
Each office had one, and all top-security documents
were supposed to be locked away overnight. Arnie felt

240

his hands getting damp as he worked the combination lock. He got the case out, placed it on the desk and opened it.

He let Kuzak examine the contents in his own time. He looked through the photographs, nodding; read the accompanying material, nodding again, then went through the pictures a second time.

'This, of course, is the he-woman of TV – Gloria Gonzales, conscience of the nation? Right?'

'Right. With her loverboy, Marcus Stallwood.'

Kuzak stood sucking the knuckles of his left hand. He was frowning. 'What I don't get, Arnie, is why you put a P.I. on your own client?'

'I thought you'd get round to asking me that.' He lowered his voice. 'I'm afraid it was Roxanne – she boobed. When I said I wanted the husband tailed, she thought I meant the wife. For God's sake, don't let on to Leland or Douglas.'

'Damn right I won't. That sort of mistake's practically a capital offence in a law firm.'

Arnie then described in detail the meeting in the Polo Lounge, and the subsequent events on the drive back to the office.

'You sure it was the same car as in the picture? A Porsche?' Kuzak asked.

'Ninety-five per cent sure. Though I didn't make the connection until after the car had gone. But it was a personalised number. MS 1. Same as in the picture.'

Kuzak nodded. It was past five and the office was about as lively as the City Morgue. 'Let's get some coffee from the machine, then I'll buy you a drink.'

They found Roxanne busy arranging and rearranging

bits of stationery on her desk. 'You guys going home soon?'

'Why, you got a date and wanna be left alone?' said Kuzak.

She gave him a brilliant smile. 'Alone with two of the most desirable bachelors in the US of A! I should be so lucky!'

They got their coffee and sat down again. Kuzak said, 'I got an idea. We make an appointment tomorrow morning to see Douglas. Then we take him the two cases. Explain everything – although we can let Roxanne off the hook by saying it was Sherwoods that goofed. And we get him to give an absolute undertaking that there will be no recriminations. But with the state of the office, I don't suppose even Douglas will have much appetite for a blood bath . . .'

There was a faint tap on the door. Arnie called out and Roxanne's face appeared. 'Sorry, guys. But there's someone outside to see you, Arnie. He doesn't have an appointment – says his name's David Hughes.'

'Did he say what it's about?'

'Well not really. But he said it was important.'

'Important for him, no doubt – not for me.'

Kuzak said, 'I'll leave you to it.' He was halfway between the desk and the door, when the man came in.

He was tall and well-built, wearing a beautifully fitting tan linen suit and a white silk polo-necked sweater, with a bright yellow silk handkerchief in his breast pocket. His hair was blond turning to grey and he had a thin, carefully-shaved moustache. Arnie remembered thinking how the man had the kind of good looks that went out with Errol Flynn. Except he'd hardly mind since he was no film actor. He came in and closed the door, then took a step forward. He had a gun in his hand.

Suddenly Arnie realised who he was. Not a stranger called David Hughes but someone whom he felt he knew extremely well, despite this being their first meeting. The man was Marcus Stallwood.

The weapon had appeared as though by sleight of hand. Stallwood obviously knew how to use it; and judging by Stuart Markowitz's probing into his financial affairs, he'd probably had quite a lot of practical experience with firearms.

It was a short-muzzled pistol – probably a .38, Arnie guessed – and small enough to fit in his pocket. The barrel was levelled at just below Arnie's stomach; and the hand that held the gun was as steady as if it were made of stone.

'What can I do for you?' Arnie said automatically, only his voice sounded to him like a rasping squeak.

Kuzak remained standing, about four feet from the man, his face taut, but otherwise without expression.

The man said, 'You know what I've come for, Becker.' It was a statement, not a question. 'Putting a tail on Gloria is one matter. She had it coming to her, trying to set up her old man as an adulterer while she played the whited sepulchre. Taking photographs which could be used to blackmail is quite another.'

Arnie found himself wondering why Stallwood had come himself, and alone – why he hadn't sent some henchman. Unless it was the kind of job he wasn't prepared to delegate to anyone – a secret he could only afford to share with Gloria . . . and with Arnie.

Stallwood continued. 'Me, I don't go for that kind of stuff. When you included me in those pictures, you crossed the line, bright boy. You got a reputation to protect – fine! But I got a reputation too. And you know how I protect it? By making sure that driftwood like you don't pull a stunt like this one and get away with it.'

If he was worried by the presence of Kuzak, he wasn't showing it. He didn't even seem to look at Kuzak. He said, 'I want all the prints of the photographs and the negatives.'

Arnie, who was still sitting, pushed the open Samsonite case across the desk. 'It's all there – except the negatives. They're with the P.I. agency.'

'Call them. Have them ready for you to pick up.'

Arnie looked at his watch. Almost 5.30. 'They may be closed.'

'Call them. Make sure they're not closed.'

Arnie picked up the phone and dialled the number. The office was up in Pasadena. He said, 'Mr Lennox, please. It's Arnold Becker, of McKenzie Brackman.' There was a pause. Kuzak moved a little closer to the wall, between Arnie and Marcus Stallwood.

'Hello? He's not there?' He glanced at Stallwood. 'This is very urgent. I want to come by as soon as possible and collect all the negatives for the pics you sent over yesterday morning.' A pause. 'Yes? There'll be no problem? Right. I'll bring my I.D., don't worry.'

He put down the phone and noticed that the receiver was slippery with sweat. But Arnie was reasonably proud of how he'd handled the call. Had there been a quaver in his voice? He looked to Kuzak for a sign of approval; but Kuzak's eyes were on Stallwood and the gun.

Stallwood caught his glance. 'Me, I use a gun like a precision instrument. Six rounds and only the last one kills. That way, I kill you more than once.' As he spoke, he licked his lips and his tongue was a small, grey-white sliver. 'Have you a car here?' he asked.

Arnie shook his head.

Stallwood turned to Kuzak. 'You?'

Kuzak shook his head. 'Nix.'

The man seemed to deliberate for a moment. It was unusual for professional people not to have a car in L.A. – if they were telling him the truth, that is.

'One of you is going to drive. If you attempt any manoeuvre in order to attract attention, I will first shoot you in the kneecaps, then in the groin.' He looked at his watch. 'You will each walk a little in front of me . . .'

As he spoke the door flew open and what looked like some huge oriental headpiece loomed up over Stallwood's head, then came crashing down on to his shoulders, and there was a terrible ear-cracking explosion that seemed to blow the office empty of air.

Arnie had thrown himself flat behind the desk. From where he lay he could see Kuzak wrestling with Stallwood, who had the big yellow basket from the front hall jammed down over his head. Above them both towered Roxanne, furious, determined, magnificent – laying into Stallwood with both high-heels in turn, until

Kuzak had managed to wrest the gun out of the man's hand.

'You were listening at the door, Rox,' Kuzak nodded grimly. 'I should put you over my knee and spank you for that.'

'Come back to my place!'

Arnie had hauled himself up and was dialling the police.

Later they found the spent bullet had entered the desk and drilled a hole through a whole card-index of past clients. He wondered if he ought to make a duplicate or frame them above his desk.

He looked at Kuzak. 'How are we gonna tell Leland and Stuart? They're supposed to be taking it easy now they're out of hospital.'

'They'll love it. It's publicity. And without publicity in this town, you're dead! Even Leland McKenzie knows that – although he'd never admit it.'

'Long live McKenzie Brackman,' Arnie said, and went out to get a cup of iced water.

24

A Celebration

Leland McKenzie returned to the office after two weeks at home, in good time to preside over the firm during the storm of scandal which blew up over Gloria Gonzales and her gangster lover, Marcus Stallwood. Leland grumbled disapprovingly and talked a lot about integrity and 'falling standards'; but in secret he was enjoying the limelight hugely.

On the Friday after Leland's return there was a buffet lunch party in the office, organised by Roxanne whose picture had appeared on several magazine covers, following her heroic rescue of her colleagues; she had even been invited on to three chat shows to talk about self-defence for women but, as she said modestly, 'It wasn't self-defence, just common-sense.'

Both Leland and Stuart, looking rather pale, had been told not to drink but Arnie would have none of it. 'To hell with it!' he said, pouring out flutes of champagne for them. 'It isn't every day we celebrate your return from the dead, or at least from the hospital.'

'Speak for yourself,' grunted Leland. 'It isn't every day you get shot at by a hoodlum.'

'Did you hear, Marcus Stallwood was indicted by a grand jury on five counts of fraud, grand larceny, expropriation of public funds and tax evasion?' Stuart said. 'He was finally released on bail, in the sum of five million dollars. He also faces a second indictment, of attempted murder.'

Stuart and Ann had been tearfully and totally reconciled – not least because Stuart's exhaustive researches had led to Marcus Stallwood's indictment; Ann now understood why his meetings with Emily had to be confidential and that they had been genuinely for his work – high-pressure work, *cordon bleu* style. No more *filet mignon* for Stuart, on his latest strict diet. Plain boiled fish was on his menu now. Ann put her arm around Stuart, deftly removing the champagne glass from his hand. 'Now, darling, you know what the doctor said,' she murmured.

Becker raised his eyebrows. Marital devotion seemed to mean deprivation of life's few lasting pleasures.

'Did you hear about Gloria Gonzales?' he asked. 'She's been destroyed by all that scalding publicity. Her show's been pulled; all the advertisers dropped out.'

'Dreadful woman,' Ann said. 'Not that I ever watched her show. Now, did you see the newspapers this morning? About that rock star who was involved in your drugs case?'

Victor Sifuentes joined them. He had just been invited to serve as an unpaid adviser for the A.C.C.L. 'I said that girl wasn't thirteen, didn't I? No-one could have seriously believed that.'

Graham Grubb, a.k.a. Adrian Calvados, had been found not guilty of the sex charge, when it was proved that Andromeda Fulton – born Miranda Gaunt – was already nineteen years old at the time of the beach party. Her much vaunted age of 13 was just hype. But on the first two counts Calvados was sent to jail for ninety days – all of which boosted Andromeda's record sales by nearly twenty per cent.

Candice and Jayne were passing around platters of canapés. Usually they chattered endlessly but today they both seemed rather subdued and silent. Arnie made his usual joking remarks to them but they didn't respond.

Leland drew Douglas into a corner. 'Have you got any further in your investigations about the head-hunting?'

He was reaching out for an asparagus roll when Candice dropped the plate. Shards of china and bits of food flew everywhere. Everyone stopped talking. Candice burst into tears. Jayne rushed to her and started to clear up the mess. Candice grasped her arm. 'We must tell them. It's not fair.'

'Tell us what?' asked Douglas, glaring at the disruption.

The girls tearfully explained that they'd both been offered double their present salary if they went to work with Radcliffe, Noach and Williams. McKenzie, in a burst of heady generosity to celebrate his recovery, instantly promised he would not only double their salary but pay them a bit more on top if they would stay. They went clattering off in their high heels, twittering with excitement as though they'd landed a screen test.

Douglas felt quite foolish for having wasted so much time suspecting his colleagues of treachery. All those times he had noticed them leaving or arriving in pairs! However, he kept his feelings to himself.

'Well, I guess I'd better keep healthy,' said Leland. 'The minute I turn my back, look what happens to the partnership.'

Postscript

Boris Grodek, a.k.a. Yevgeny Oblomov, was charged on two counts of causing a public nuisance, was directed to be of good character and given a conditional discharge for twelve months – a verdict which he loudly denounced as 'character assassination'.

About this time Kuzak and Abby were having an ice cream in the Italian store next to the office. 'Funny thing is,' Abby said, 'I rather admire the old rogue.'

'Who?'

'The Count. The Prince. The phoney. Whatever you like. I mean, he's just *not like anyone I've ever met before*!'

'I won't argue with that, Abby. But does this mean you're getting soft on him? Want to look after him, clean his apartment and pay the bills and get the vodka chilled to just the right temperature . . . ?'

'No. But you have to admit, he is rather *sweet*?'

Kuzak almost choked. 'Abby, whatever else he is, our bogus Count most certainly is *not* sweet. He is what the legal profession calls a "chronic and vexatious litigator". In other words, a pain in the ass.'

He was partially proved right when it was announced that the *Pacific Review* prudently decided against pursuing the Russian for damages. However, it was not long before he was to appear in an L.A. civil court, trying to sue the U.S. representative of an Israeli publishing house which he claimed had issued a pirated edition of *The Practical Jokes of J. V. Stalin*. He did not use the firm of McKenzie Brackman, but represented himself. He lost.

*

Gloria eventually married a Brazilian millionaire who had his own TV station. Her ex-husband, Mort Smellie, surfaced in the Far East, as a PR man for a string of casinos in the former Portuguese colony of Macao, off the Chinese mainland.

Emily Stallwood divorced Marcus – without recourse to either Arnie Becker or Stuart Markowitz – and she later went to England where she married a gentleman farmer with a small stately home near Cirencester, Gloucestershire.

*

That left Arnie Becker. On that first Saturday, after he'd found himself looking down the mouth of Stallwood's gun, he decided to have a quiet evening at home. He'd got himself a six-pack of German beer and was settling down to watch a video. His hand was just reaching out for the telephone, to order a pizza, when it rang. He let it ring. It went on and on. Then it stopped. He opened one of the cans of beer.

A FAIR TRIAL

CHARLES BUTLER

Chuck Carlton, a young and successful advertising executive, has a head-on collision with another car, killing a mother and her son. When a journalist finds out that Carlton had committed a drink-driving offence only recently, the media close in for the kill. Kuzak, called on to defend Carlton, fights to keep his mind fixed on the facts of the case, determined that his client should have a fair trial.

Price: £3.99
ISBN: 1 85283 606 7

Boxtree will be publishing 2 more LA Law novels in November 1991.